MAMA CAN'T RAISE NO MAN

Robyn Travis

First published in the United Kingdom by:
OWN IT! Entertainment Ltd
in Hardback: 9780995458918

Company Registeration Number: 09154978

Paperback ISBN: 9780995458949

Book Jacket Design: James Nunn

WWW.OWNIT.LONDON

Dedicated to all the single parents out there forced to raise their children alone the best way they know how.

COURT TRANSCRIPT

Mr Ricketts, please stand.

On the 27th of November police were called to an address on Road Man Avenue just down the road from Broadwater Farm estate in Tottenham to investigate a case of domestic violence. On arrival they were confronted by an altercation between you, the mother of your children and her male friend for which you were arrested and subsequently charged with on count of common assault against Candice Honeyghan. There was also an additional charge of grievous bodily harm on a... Mr Tyrone Campbell. As if that wasn't bad enough, on searching your parked vehicle, the officers at the scene discovered £900 pounds in cash, 46 wraps of heroin, weighing a total of 14.2 grams and 15 wraps of cocaine weighing…. err… 5.4 grams.

Despite the weight of evidence against you, you refused to take responsibility when interviewed. Instead you repeatedly claimed that the drugs were not yours. However you then entered a last minute guilty plea, which leads me to conclude that you are finally willing to own up and take responsibility for your actions in light of the overwhelming evidence against you.

Mr Ricketts, there is no doubt in my mind that the drugs were yours and that you did indeed intend to sell them for profit. Your previous history shows that this is an offence that you are no stranger to. In fact, I myself sentenced you for intent to supply three years ago. This leaves me to conclude that you have absolutely no respect for the law and that you continue to be one of the parasites who prey on the young and vulnerable of our society by plying them with recreational poison for your own profitable gain.

I have taken into consideration the character references presented, which portray you as a good parent and a positive contributor to the community. While there are several testimonials in regards to the work you have done to get youth off the street by involving them with the local football team on Broadwater Farm, I'm afraid I'm not at all convinced that you are a changed man. All I see standing here infront of me is the same Duane Ricketts that stood before me three years ago and you certainly bear no resemblance to the 'street saint' that you're portrayed to be in these testimonies I have before me.

You knew full well when supplying these drugs, Mr Ricketts, that possession with the intent to supply is a serious offence and carries a prison sentence. If you were the great father you and others claim, surely, you would have known the impact that a custodial sentence would have on your children given the fact that you are now going to be absent from their lives for a significant amount of time. Immediate custody is inevitable for offences of this gravity.

Mr Ricketts, I'd also urge you to take a look at your mother! To look long and hard at what this is doing to the poor woman. You've been convicted 3 times in your 24 years of living. It's been an ongoing occurrence since the tender age of 15. Having said that, it would be remiss not to acknowledge that this string of convictions must surely be, in part at least, a reflection of the way you were raised. Ms Ricketts, I can't begin to fathom why you allowed your son out there on the streets from the age of 15? Surely any decent parent would've made sure that their child was in the house by a reasonable hour.

If you had control of your son at a much earlier age Ms Ricketts, I dare say he wouldn't have been able to get into trouble. While Mr Ricketts is responsible for his own actions, you Ms Ricketts must also take responsibility for the role you did or didn't play as his parent.

Ms Ricketts as a mother myself, it is hard for me to have to pass sentence on your son whilst you're so tearful. I'm sure you're plagued with shame and pain. But as a Judge in the court of law my only concern is that the law is upheld as it should be.

Mr Ricketts my personal opinion is that you deserve nothing less but the full force of the law. However I must take your guilty plea into consideration. Your sentence will be a total of

44 months imprisonment. You will serve at least half of that sentence before being released on licence, depending on your behaviour. That is the sentence of the court. Good day.

Son,

How are you keeping? I know it's not easy right now, but you've been through this before and you're strong enough to go through it again. You've got to be strong, son.

How are they treating you? I hope you're not getting into any arguments with the prison guards. Don't go making things harder for yourself. Please, just try and keep peace with them. Even if they try to wind you up, stay calm. You know they would love nothing more than to make you serve your full sentence and then some. You can't let them get to you in the way they did last time. Deal with it like a man.

As for that judge that sentenced you, don't pay her no mind. She's too rude. 'Bout she feels my grief. Trust me son I had to pray on the spot and ask the good Lord to give me strength or else I would have ended up in there with you. Are you eating well? Do you need me to send some money? Have you got a phonecard? Call me if you need anything.

Mum xxx

P.S. I saw Pastor Benjamin, you remember, my old preacher from Dalston who always tried to get you to come church. I let him know what's going on. So last Sunday he told the whole congregation, that you're back in there and to pray for you. Everyone's got you in their prayers son. Some of them even want to come and visit to pray with you. What shall I tell them? They've been praying about my high blood pressure. But Pastor Ben says that praying for me alone won't bring my blood pressure down. They have to pray for you too.

Yo, D

Wha' gwan, my Nigg?

Man don't even know what to say right about now. Shit just seems to always be peak for you. How is it that every time I come out the can you end up going in? Some mickey mouse business. I've only been on road like what, 5 weeks.

Us man came down court the other day to support you. But you looked well pissed my brudda. I doubt you even noticed us man jamming in the gallery. I've never seen you look so stressed, that screwface you gave the judge was emotional.

I know you're screwing right now, but don't watch no face. All the main man dem on road are out ere saying 'Ricketts is still a real G' and free my N##ga Ricks' cos of the way you dealt with the case. Obviously it's standard, real niggas don't snitch. But still.

All I can say is that you're one loyal brudda fam. Cah if it was me I would be getting onto my younger telling him to step up and own up to the food. You're good bruv, not me though I ain't trying to catch a case for a 3rd time. I only just touch road I ain't riding no bird again cuz. No way my Nigg not for nothing or no-one. Look how much of the man dem are sitting on a IPP! But you do your thing my G. I can't knock you, you held it down for dem man. So if you need help bussin' case on that next ting, just say the word and I'll pass it on.

On a next tip though my brudda. I see the way you was moving out here, it was different. You proper tried to change up your life and come off the road ting. You made that ish look easy, I rate that. I'm gonna have to try take a take leaf outta your book still. But in the meantime a man gotta eat. We've been on road for years, but this road life's dead now. And my second yute is getting big quick fast. I'm gonna try do things the way that you tried to. I need to go look a job before I get itchy fingers. One that works round my probation. It's time for man to try and leggo this road ting for good and go legit. But legit ain't easy darg, you know this. If it was, a changed man like you wouldn't be back in there. Ah-lie, fam?

Yeah, and I heard about the fuckery your baby mudda Candy is gwarning with. You know I feel your pain on that one my G. I don't know what makes these bitches think they can just stop a brudda from seeing his own yute. KMT. All I know is if I ever catch my first baby mother Selina walking on road with my yute I'm looking to crack her jaw. Call me a woman beater I don't care my nigga.

My son's gonna be 8 soon and I ain't seen him since he was four. No address. No number. No nothing. That shit ain't right. Why didn't you show man that Candy stopped you from seeing them? You never told me that fam. That shit must really be pissing you off in there. I bet you never thought your baby mother was one of them fucked-up type ah bitches like Selina.

I told you from day one bruv, you can't be wifing off these hood-rat bitches. They're just like us man on road, cold fucking hearted.

Anyway, try an keep your head up but your head down at the same time. You know the ting already.

Roll easy and holla if you need to. You know I always got you and vice versa.

One Love, One Arda

Redz

Duane, bruv, WTF man?

How you gonna change from 'not guilty' to 'guilty' at the last minute and how you manage to end up back in there for drugs?

Guilty? So basically you lied to everyone then. Even to yourself. What happened to all that talk last Christmas 'bout going legit? You looked me dead in the face and said, "Sis I'm never going jail again. New year, new me. No matter how hard times get I'll never hustle again, swear down" you said."

You said that Imani and Justice are more important to you than the roads. Didn't you say that? I proper believed you as well. It come like I can't believe a single word you say. You're not a man of your word.

I'm still not buying that domestic violence charge against you, tho. I don't believe that crap. I know my brother wouldn't box down no girl.

But when it comes to drugs, I just can't tell with you.
I don't know what to believe anymore. Your so-called friends are tryna tell me the drugs weren't yours, that you're just keeping it real. Forget keeping it real, bruv. You got kids to think about. Keep it real to them. How are you gonna tell them why you weren't there for another two years of their lives because you were 'keeping it real'? What kind of example are you setting to Imani as a man? He worships you, but if you keep disappearing out of his life he'll end up dissing you.

You're supposed to be my big brother, D, but sometimes, I swear, it feels like I'm the older one. You're like - a little big brother.
I always got to take care of you and your business when you're behind bars. I can't be too mad cos you do always have my back. Anyway I'm here as per usual and I still love you Big 'ead. Stay out of trouble.

Marissa

Dear Mr Ricketts

I'm afraid I've got some bad news for you.

Your appeal against the length of your sentence, based on the perceived bias by the judge, has been turned down. If I might say so as your solicitor, your x-rated outburst following the sentencing wasn't helpful to your cause.

I understand your sense of anger and injustice after the judge's closing remarks, but you have to learn to control your temper in a court of law.

Abuse to judges doesn't go down well with other judges. I still believe that an appeal for a non-custodial sentence based on your outstanding contribution to the local community would have been a better option, even though the odds were always going to be against you.

You are due in court on the 7th October pending your case of GBH. I hope you will listen to my advice this time round and try to refrain from losing your temper. If you don't you will lose in court. Many things will come out in the case about your relationship, which you will no doubt find unpleasant. But may I be as bold as to suggest that you sit on your hands and bite your tongue throughout the proceedings. Let your barrister take the strain.

I shall be in touch if need be. Good luck in court.
Sincerely

M.J. Greaves

Solicitor at law

Son,

Did you get my first letter?

I wrote to you about two weeks ago and I still haven't heard back from you. What's the matter? Didn't you get it? Have you forgotten how to write? Or are you trying to help raise my blood pressure? Don't forget, I'm still your mum. You know how I worry already. I need to know that you are alright. I know what you're going through is hard, I get that. But please let me know how things are. Please. Maybe I can help. Maybe I can't. But you know what they say, a trouble shared is a trouble halved, no man is an island.

Hope you're well, son, I'm waiting for your letter.

Mum

P.S. Don't forget to pray!

D,

I swear I'm gonna box that dry 'ed gyal down, y'know. Your baby mother's sister that is! How could this stink nappy-head, crusty face dutty gyal come and knock down my door at 7 in the morning? On a Saturday! Can you believe the cheek of this hoodrat?

I thought it was them Jehovah Witnesses at first 'till I see this chick, with a bundle of weave on her head, walking away from my yard shouting off her lips 'bout the Ricketts family ain't shit - in or out of jail. I swear down, D, I wanted to take off my slippers and go and fix the bitch up, but it might have made things worse for you. So I just 'llowed her to run up her gums.

As I come down the stairs I see one letter without an envelope by my door. I only read the first sentence. Then I clocked the facety gyal must be wanting me to send it to you like my names friggin postman Pat. Facety rarseclart. KMT. Anyway, I didn't read through your business, but I attached her letter to mine so you can hear what the hood rat's saying.

Don't let her letter draw you out, bruv. You know what Lorna's like.

Rissa Xxx

Duane, Duane,

Tell me something…

What is it about your family? Why is it your family love to make out that you're some type of angels? Especially that little nappy head sister of yours, the bitch can't even tie her hair in a bun.

You know u ain't no saint. Acting like your shit don't stink. You didn't really think you could put your hand on my lil' sister and get away with it did you? How dare you? Are you mad bruv? Who the hell do you think you are? Let me tell you something, prick, you ain't no one and you must be crazy if you think you're gonna get away with that shit. I'm gonna make you pay. And I know big men who will gladly fuck your shit up. You must have lost your mind when you put your hands on her.

My sister's name ain't Rihanna, rude bwoy. I can't stand men like you, or should I say boys like you. The problem is that you lot think you run tings. I blame your mum for your slackness. She never taught you no better. She never raised no man. If she did you would've known how to treat a lady.

Here's the thing Duane - real men don't put their hands on women. But don't worry, when my niece and nephew grow up I'm gonna let them know how much of a wasteman their dad really is.

On a positive note, at least you're back home where you belong - in a cage. You're an animal. And the longer we can keep you behind bars the better. See you in court you little woman beater.

Lorna

Yo, big brudda,

Nothing but love for the way you had my back. You know you didn't have to do that for me, but man really appreciate it all the same. You're my brother for life. Brother from another mother, The realist brudda alive. I want you to know dat. I know you're probably still vex with man, but what else can I say? Man got caught slippin'. God knows, big brudda, if I had known you was coming back that night, I would've never fast-up myself and baited up your shit like that. My bad, cuz, my bad.

Whatever it takes I'm gonna make it up to you, my G. Just say the word. What's done is done already, but just know that I'm already putting in that work to make sure you don't have to ride any extra time. I can't ever pay you back for this one, but try-know G, when you land road, you're gonna be nice for paper.

And what's this talk I'm hearing on road? Man are saying you Mayweathered your baby mother and her new pen pal? I know you don't get down like that, M.O.E for life. Real talk. Man will make sure you buss that case as well.

One arda (M.O.E)

ATM

Duane,

Cha, how you manage to go jail a third time?

Three times! What, you love man or something? If you knew how much it buns me to know seh you get lock up again.

What happened this time? You're always finding yourself in these situations. Why you so angry? What's up with you? What's going on in that head of yours?

You can't keep living like this y'know. You need to check yourself before you wreck yourself. I can't lie, Duane, I'm really disappointed to hear your back in there. But you're my nephew so I love you all the same.

Why did you do it?

Aunty Jan-Jan

Bro,

Still haven't heard from you.

Why you acting up for? You're vex cos of what I said in my 1st letter innit? Well I don't business no more D, it had to be said. At first I thought you weren't getting my letters, but even mum's telling me you're not replying. I phoned the prison to find out if you were on the block or whether they shipped you out.

So now I'm wondering if you're opening your mail. What's going on? I saw your bredrin Redz in Bruce Grove. Your mates looking silly hench. Even his muscles got muscles, but he's still got dem match-stick legs though. Have you seen him since he come out?

He kept asking about you. He says you haven't replied to him nei-ther. He wanted to know how you were and how you and Candy are getting along and if there was anything he could do to help. You know I don't really like most of your bredrins but you see Redz he's proper bless, he's always got you. Anyway, I hope you open this letter because I've got some bad news for you.

I've been opening all your letters. There was one from UPS saying that they're terminating your employment with immediate effect. They must have seen the article in the Tottenham Journal about you going jail. Everybody's talking about it. There was a big picture of you on the front page. You didn't look too happy in it. 'SO-CALLED COMMUNITY WORKER'S DRUGS SHAME' didn't help neither. According to their letter, you have breached the terms of your UPS contract by going jail.

I went down to the depot to talk to them. I tried my best to explain that it isn't your fault that you're locked up and that it wasn't your drugs. But they weren't having a bar of it. So, honestly speaking bro, I'd say that you've lost that job. Don't worry about it though, you'll bounce back when you come out.

And that's not all. The council have sent you an eviction notice. According to them they've been watching the flat for ages and the neighbours say they've seen you dealing drugs from that address. I went down to the housing and tried to reason with them, but they're not having a bar of it either bruv. They say that dealing drugs from the property is against housing rules and results in an automatic eviction. You've got until the end of the month to clear all your stuff out before the bailiffs come and chuck it out.

Don't stress nothing though bruv, you're not on your own. I've got your back.

xxxx

P.S. What do you want me to do about all your stuff in the yard?

Yo my brudda,

I need a favour ASAP, like yesterday! I need you to shout YOU
KNOW WHO for me, and tell him 'Don't go nowhere near my
yard' cos it's flames right now.

I'm easy bro just in ere riding my bird as we do, you know how it
go already, not much more to it. Chat to my yute for me - make
sure you're not on no long ting. Even though I'm fucking pissed with
him I can't have him getting bagged too, ya get me my darg. And, nah,
I didn't see you in court, but good looking out my G.

Bless up, L.O.E Loyalty Over Everything

Duane

P.S. Don't call my baby mother a bitch again! What happened is
between me and her. Only I got the right to call her a bitch and you
ain't never heard me say that. So don't diss the ting again. And don't
let anyone know that you've heard from me.

Bless

Hey bro,

I got your messages, sorry I missed your calls.

Tell me you never box down my bredrin, Duane? And please tell me my godchildren didn't have to witness all of this drama, I beg. You two were perfect for each other. Just perfect. Until you fucked her over. Why did you have to go fuck it up?

Right now I'm pissed with you and Cands, cos you're both my bredrins and none of you ain't thinking about the twins. So what are you saying? What happened exactly? Since I've come back to London Candy's had her phone off, so I can't get her side of the story. I'm going round there this evening to make sure they are all well and I'll write you tomorrow to fill you in.

I'm not gonna take sides, Duane, you know I wouldn't do that. Regardless of what happened you're still my boy, but Candy's still my girl, and right now I'm just worried for the both of you.

Teah

Duane,

So you can respond to your friends' letters, huh? But you can't even contact your own mother. You see you....

You're just like your father.

Look how long I've been writing, telling you I'm worried. It's like you love putting your pride and friends before your own family. This same family who cleans up behind you every time you mess tings up. I don't see your friends sending you money it's me. You're too damn ungrateful.

Just like your father.

I never raised you like this. You don't take no responsibility for your actions like a real man would.

Just like your father.

What happened to the sweet little boy I used to love? Now look, you're starting to favour your puppa and you have adopted many of his stink ways. You think I don't see how you've become a little womaniser?

Just like your father.

I never raised you like this Duane. You're breaking my heart. I expected you to go so far in life. All I've ever wanted is the best for you, son, but instead you're there ignoring me like I'm one of these little fast-arse girls ringing down your phone, that you haven't got the time of day for.

Just like your father.

I know I'm not the best mother. I can admit that much. But, unlike your father, I've never abandoned you. I've made my mistakes but that doesn't give you the right to treat me like this. Come better than that. I'm not gonna run you down, Duane. If you don't write me back this time I'm gonna do to you what you've always done to me and turn my back on you.

I didn't think the day would come when I would have to say your Uncle Leroy might be right for once. He said mama can't raise no man. I never thought I would have to say you are wutless bwoy...

Just like your father.

Mum

Duane,

It's Candy… she's gone… THEY'VE gone.

I went round there yesterday, like I said I would, but nobody was there. They've proper gone ghost. Vanished. Disappeared. On my life Duane this ain't a good look. When I say everything's gone I mean EVERYTHING - the furniture, the kids' push-bikes and even the curtains… all gone.

What have you done? Did you threaten her or something? What did you say to her to make her go? Where do you think she could have gone ? And what about the kids? They can't just up and leave like that in the middle of a school term. I talked to the neighbours. Nobody seems to know where she's at. Nobody. You know how it is on these mix-up estates. Everyone wants to be in your business but nobody wants to talk up the tings when you need some help. Nobody ain't saying nothing. I've been belling down her phone but still haven't been able to get through. What shall I do, Duane? Shall I call feds? What do you want me to do? Phone me.

Teah

TELEPHONE CALL: DUANE TO REDZ

DUANE
Yo my brudda it's D

REDZ
D? D who?

DUANE
Oi Don't take the piss,
it's your day 1 CO-D.

REDZ
Ahh, D, sorry I should've recognised
it was a prison number. What's good, G?
Ain't heard from you in a minute.

DUANE
Fuck-alls good right about now.
I need you to do sutin for me like yesterday.

REDZ
Anything my darg. What, you want me
to get one of the young bucks to lick
someone down for you?

DUANE
NO, fuck all that bait talk, Red.
Come better than that, fam.
Y'know babylon record these convos.

REDZ
Ahhhh shit, sorry fam, true say
I just woke up and dat.

DUANE
Cool, say nuttin.
Quick ting before my credit dun out.
I need you to go to my yutes dem

school and see if their Mum's moved
them out.

REDZ
What?

DUANE
Yeah, mad-ting I just got word from
someone that Candy's bussed out
with my yutes. I'm trying to hold it
down still but I can't front it's getting to
me.. Find out where they're at, G, I beg.
Strictly Malcolm X mentality
on this one, yeah? I can't do shit
from in here so just do what you can.

REDZ
Say no more family tree. I Got you!

DUANE
Oh and one more thing, tell YOU
KNOW WHO to fucking behave himself. His
name's ringing bells in here. Every time I
come out my cell for sosh I'm hearing this
yute's name caught up in some drama. I
thought he was About That Money. The way my
man's moving it's like he's all About The
Mix-up. I beg youhave a word with him for me,
just tell him I said lay-low. Trust me
he don't wanna come big man jail so make
sure you tell him darg. Shit, My credits
about to die... One love brudda."

Bruv,

No disrespect, but how are you really gonna try school me about the roads now?

I'm not 14 no more, G. I know the game inside out, I'm outchea. I've never gone jail before. You're the one that's always in and out. So why you telling Redz to tell me to lay low. Lol. 'Llow me fam, they don't call me ATM for nothing - About That Money, remember? Stop stressing, I got you.

Oh yeah, on a next note, man caught one of those outta town yutes slipping. Dem same yutes you were telling me stepped to you at the funfair when you were with your kids?

No lay-lay, bruh. Man just dragged him outside and yanked him up quickly. Simple. Us man will always put in work for you, G. It's nothing. True say you're a man that's older and you looked after us man when we were proper youngers. That yute deserved to get bruck up. 'Bout he's doing the badman ting in front of your kids. Nahhh fam, he can't get away with them type of disrespect. My man had to get rubbed out quickly.

Oh yeah, and man went to a next dance and caught that other yute who shot you back in the day. Man had to done the dance then leave the dance. Ya feel me? Mans fully outchea. I'm a man of my word, G. When I said I'll make it up to you, I meant that shit. Just be easy and fall back.

Oh yeah, my yute is due to land next week, fam. Just thought I'd let you know. Bless, big bro.

ATM

ATM bruv

Who you telling to fall back? Don't forget yourself. D'you know how bait your letters are? Why the fuck are you self-snitching? Don't you think they read mans letters in here? Come better than that, lickle brudda. Don't be writing me letters running up your mouth cos you're getting paper. I'm not gonna penny it this time, but I beg you don't draw me out.

And you don't have to tell me about who you lot bruck up for me, cah right now I'm on the same wing with a bag of his bredrins. I think they got done for one shooting at carny or sutt'n. It all makes sense now why they were acting iffy around me in the gym.

You lot really didn't need to touch my yute for me. We squashed the beef when I was on road. How many times have I begged you to leave my beef alone? You're not my soldier I don't want you to have my back like that. Don't do that shit for me again, my brudda. Just do YOU. And you're a eeeeediat, lol, about 'did I Mayweather my baby mudda.' I ain't no woman beater and yeah, dem charges got dropped, so don't farse up yourself, do nuttin'.

Real talk though, calm yourself down. By the time you get this letter your first yute should've dropped. Just 'llow the hype for a bit and try getting yourself into daddy mode. Trust me, my yute, the transition ain't easy.

I can't even believe you're gonna be a dad now my lickle brudda. If it's a boy call him Duane, and if it's a girl... fuck it call her Duaney lol. Nah I'm chatting shit. Big up yourself and roll safe, baby-farda. Make sure you write me after the yute lands.

Duane

P.S. #LeggoDaRoads

Lord God, Duane,

Please tell me it's not true.

Please God, tell me it's a lie. I just bumped into one of your friends in Rigley Road market, and he come up to me and said, "Mrs Ricketts, I just come out of Pentonville prison. You hear what happened to Duane?" The boy said a couple of the inmates rushed you and you're in the hospital. What's going on, son? What the hell's going on in there? Are you okay? Are you hurt bad? I'm praying that you are alright.

I called your solicitor to find out what's happening. They said the police took you back to the prison wing this morning. I'm glad to hear that. And I'm glad to hear from your lawyer that the Crown Prosecution Service decided to drop the other charges of common assault and GBH against you. That is good news. I knew no son of mine was a woman-beater.

Your loving mother

P.S. I didn't mean what I said in that last letter when I said you're wutless and just like your father. I didn't mean it I was just vex. Oh… and I've sent you some money.

What's good Teah?

Yeah I got your letter last month but I didn't open any letters cos I didn't wanna get into nothing till after my trial. And no. Don't call no feds on Candy. I don't want my kids to get caught up in this social worker business.

Have you spoken to her yet? Did you manage to track her down? Where the fuck are my yutes? Let me know when you know wha gwarn. I need to know. And in case you didn't hear already man buss case. The brudda dropped the charges, and Cands admitted that I didn't box her down, so it's been thrown out of court. It's finished, I'm only in here for the drugs now. And even that's not what you think it is.

I bet you feel shame to know I didn't box down your best friend. And you're a mad girl, if you think I would fight a man over a woman. I'm not watching that. I just wanna see my yutes dem. Whatever she does is her business. I can't do nothing about it, it's her life innit. What type of madman do you take me for?

You've known me from day, sis. Come better than that Teah. Seriously, man. I know Candy's your home girl, but what you were saying in your letter did kinda feel like you were taking sides. I didn't even feel like writing you back at first, real talk. But you're right, if I didn't cheat on Candy we wouldn't be here now. I wish I could take back what I've done. But I can't! That don't give her the right to stop me seeing my kids though. I swear Teah if this girl's trying to take my yutes away from me for good I'll come for her.

It's true what you said Teah, me and Candy were perfect for each other but at the time man couldn't see it. I'm man enough to admit that. Maybe I needed this time behind bars to really think things through. Maybe I needed to go ghost to get my head straight. I would have preferred a little holiday in Spain myself but F it I'm 'ere innit.

I beg you if you can find her, chat to her for me please. My solicitor said by law I can talk to her now, but I would rather not. I just wanna talk to my yutes. And I know it's her facety anti-man sister up in her ears telling her not to let me see my yutes. Her sister's one badmind dysfunctional bitch. She always wanted us to break up. She's a straight man-hater. So do me a favour and see if you can sort things out with Candy so I can at least write to my yutes.

Anyway enough long talk. How's Uni? Keep up the hard work. Mad proud of you, sis. Pity, by the time you graduate from Law School I won't need you to bail me out, cah I ain't never coming here again. Dead that.

Do your thing T and we'll catch up.

Bless
Duane

D,

I'm sorry for asking you if you boxed up my bredrin. I heard people saying that and I know you got a temper when you're ready so I had to ask. I should've known better to accuse you but I know my friend is quick to lift her hand sometimes too so I just pictured the worse scenario.

I was just writing to tell you to try not to worry about your kids safety. Candy's probably just angry somewhere trying to get her head straight – she'll be back. Candy can be badmind sometimes but she ain't badmind like that. She's not the type to run away and hide with your kids and never come back – no way. Just try and be headstrong in there.

And it means a lot to hear you say your proud of me. It's not like you to have a moment and say something nice like that – so thanks bruv. It's funny cos when I'm doing my essays, I always think you would have made a sick solicitor if you took that route. You've always been like a brother to me and I want you to know I'm here if you ever wanna open up or just reason.

Anyway, I'm going back up to Brummy for my last year of uni, I gotta put my head down now. A sista gotta get them grades y'know. I got a couple of girls in the ends looking for Candy so I'll write you if anything comes up. Don't be a stranger and write me while I'm gone.
Keep your head up and don't stress too much. Wherever the kids are, they're with their Mum and you know my bredrin takes care of her kids.

Love u my brother from another.

Teah

Robyn Travis

Yo, darg

You know I got your back out here - I had to slap up one of the youngers in Farm, true he was saying Ricketts is a pum-pum. But don't watch that, I got you.

I spoke to ATM but that little nigga ain't cooling down for no-one, that yute's more hype than we were. I always see him in Wood Green at some dance, bussing champs on some hype ting and starting up beef. He's gonna get himself fucked-up soon if he carries on. But boy, y'nah that's not my problem. That nigga's your younger, not mine.

BTW I looked for your b-ms and kids dem. I ain't seen them myself but someone told me that she's living with that Tyrone Campbell brudda from H-town. Piss-take, innit. I told you from day 1 from we was in school at Gladesmore with her, not to trust Candy. No doubt dem Hackney girls are piff but you can't wife them, they can't be trusted.

Oh yeah, I see your old links the other day - remember big batty Letisha - she was asking for you. I gave her your prison number so she could write to you. I know how it goes in there you must be roasting my darg. There's no harm in a little pillow talk.

Gone again brudda from another – holla if you need anything.

Redz

Yo Teah!

Just read your letter and I'm thinking your right b. I gotta try not to stress too much, I know my kids are still eating. And I can't do much from in here.

But still this shits madding me.

Anyway, do me a favour. Don't write me back until you finish your 3rd year. If you write me before next year May I swear down I'm not responding. I'm not being funny either sis, it's all love same way but them grades ain't gonna come without hard work. So do your thing and make yourself proud.

Speak with you next year. Love T.

Duane x

Duane,

What's this I'm hearing that some guys rushed you and you ended up in hospital?!

Are you all right? Who were they? Why did they attack you? Are they going to move you from that prison?

You're still not talking to mum. Why are you treating her like that? I dunno what's going on with you two but you lot need to sort it out. You have to 'llow her, bruv, you know she don't cope too well when you're in there. Just call her once in awhile. She's hurting right now, she didn't tell me this but I know she feels it's her fault why you keep going jail. She's chatting like she's failed you somehow.

On another note Bruv, I need to get your advice on something. It's been bugging me for a little while now.

Oh yeah, send me a VO for next month. I wanna come see your big head before your bday.

Love you D, try stay out of trouble please.

Your favourite sister Marrisa X

Yo Bruv,

So the Tyrone brudda dropped the charges, huh?

I told you I got you. Are you still sure you want me to stay out of your business, yeah? Lol. I heard that the charges got dropped against you by your baby mudda. I heard one of the neighbours in Farm recorded everything and uploaded that shit on Insta, so the whole hood could see you fighting that Tyrone dude and Candy t'umping you on your head from behind. That shit got about 2000 likes before I got them to take it down. At least it's certified now the hood knows you didn't deck your b-ms.

And, my bad again cuz, I didn't know that us man moving to that yute would get you rushed in there. My bad. But try know if you want it's not a problem for us man to go back and finish off the job. Anyting ah anyting. Just say the word G. I know you're a changed man and that, but you can't have everyone out 'ere thinking you're a pussy. That shit don't look good on your CV darg.

ATM

TELEPHONE CALL: DUANE TO MARRISA

MARRISA
Hello private number...

DUANE
Yo my darg.

MARRISA
Who the hell's this? I think you got
the wrong number bruv, I ain't no-one's
darg.

DUANE
Lol you're right you're not no-one's
darg. You're a chick. So that makes
you my bitch.

MARRISA
WHAT! Your Mum's your bitch, come off my
phone you facety rarse…

HANG UP TONE

DUANE CALLS AGAIN

MARRISA
Dutty bwoy why the rarse you ringing me
chatting shit? Come off my phone and go wash
your balls you little batty bwoy, and
don't ring me back.

DUANE
Wait! Rissa, it's me, man.

MARRISA
Duane? You're an eeeediat! Why you
pranking me? And how you calling me

after 10? Ain't you meant to be on
lock-down?

DUANE

Don't ask big-man no questions. Nah, my
cell mate's got a mobile in here and he let
me use it still. Firstly, how's my niece?

MARRISA

You're a joker. Destiny is fine, got a little
cold at the moment but she's good.

DUANE

Cool, tell her Uncle D loves her. Secondly,
I hope you're good. Thirdly, I got all of
your previous letters.

MARRISA TRIES TO INTERRUPT

'Llow writing me
a hundred and one questions about why
I'm back in here. Don't you think I know
I fucked up? You think I really need to
hear the 411 from you as well? This
ain't no talk show Jeremy.

MARISSA

Shuttup you fool **[Laughing]**. If your arse
didn't keep going to jail every five
minutes then maybe I wouldn't need to be on
such a need to know.

DUANE

I swear you think you're my girl sometimes
[Laughing]. Anyway, how's Mum?

MARISSA

Mum's ok. She's hurt that you won't reply

to her letters though. Calling my phone
every minute: "Have you heard from Duane?".
But you know Mum, she just gets on with
it. She nearly had a heart attack when
she heard you got rushed. Are you OK now?

DUANE

Yeah sis. That beating was a minor. Mum's
licks made man 'ard bodied - ya get me?
I only went hospital because I wanted to
get out of the jail for a minute. Told
them it was worse than what it was.
Minor tings sis come on I've been shot
before, come jail before and rushed bare
times, this shit don't even bother me
no more. Have you heard from my kids?
I heard that Candy's kicked out and gone
back to live in Hackney with some east gee-
zer.

MARISSA

Nah, bro, I haven't seen Candy or the
kids since they stopped you from seeing
them last year. Destiny keeps asking for
them aswell she really misses her cousins.

DUANE

I know its peak

MARRISA

You need to go to court when you come
out and fight to get custody. What she's
doing is fucked up.

DUANE

Nah fuck all that sis, I know nuff man
who can't see their yutes. Why the fuck
am I going to court to fight for what I
made? And to top it off I ain't got money

for all them legal fees. Man don't get no
legal aid to fight this. The system's
fucked for man. Worse still I got a
criminal record. I'll just be wasting
money I don't have. Anyway I don't
wanna talk about that right now.

MARRISA
I did see her yam-out head sister
Lorna at the hairdressers in Bruce Grove
last week. Looks like she's bleaching or
something. How's this girl got 5 kids
for 6 different baby fathers? As much as
I hate her guts I will try and chat to her
for you so you can at least get
through to your kids.

DUANE
Please. If you can ask Lorna to give
me an address.. By the way, don't worry about
my stuff in the flat I'll just rebuild my life
when I land road again. Thanks for trying to
save my job and flat sis. Oh yeah before I go
what's this thing you've been wanting to tell
me but haven't had the time?

MARRISA
It's just my baby father acting up

DUANE
What? He didn't put his hand on you did he

Marrisa
Nah, it's nothing like that. I don't want to
waste your credit, I'll write to you.

DUANE
Cool, cool, I'll send you a VO but don't
be coming here giving me no lectures on the

visit cos I'll just ask the screws to send me back to my cell. I always tell you, you don't understand what it's like to be a man out ere, and I ain't got the time to explain. I'm gone. Love you big nose.

MARRISA
Wateva big head, don't drop the soap, and I'll see you soon, love you too big ed."

Aunty J,

How you gonna come at me like that? You're meant to know I don't hit gyal. Wasn't it you that use to ruff me up anytime mum told you I hit Marrisa?

So you're gonna believe whatever it is you've heard without asking me, yeah? You're just as bad as everyone else then. Almost as bad as the police. I guess I'm guilty, until proven innocent! KMT.

Remember what got me in here. She's the one who stopped me from seeing my kids. I went there on some peace talk then it just kicked off. Now look, look how long I ain't seen my kids for Aunty! I miss them. It's like Candy's been brainwashed. She just turned wicked over-night.

I only went to this girl's yard cos I wanted to see my yutes. But when I've got there now, some next brudda's standing there, chatting to her at the front door. I stood next to who she was chatting to she just stops smiling and slams the door in me and this random brudda's face.

So I knocked on the door and said: "I wanna see my kids, I'm not here to argue with you." Then she try tell me to just go. I started banging the door and then the brudda put his hand on me and I sort of pushed me back, so I flipped on him.

Candy comes out the yard like superwoman trying to save homeboy. She jumped on me and grabbed me by the neck, so I dashed her off me. Honestly, I did not know it was her on my back until I dashed her. As I went to pick her up, police come and arrested me on the spot saying I punched her in the eye. Don't ask me how she got a black eye, maybe she landed on her face. I dunno. I didn't do it. And, I'm vex that you could've thought that I would box up my baby mum. Over what, Aunty? she's still the mother of my kids.

Duane

Nephew,

I hear what you're saying but you're still missing my point.

Because if you were doing what you were meant to be doing you wouldn't be in this drama.

You're not living right. Everything about you is mix up. And you need to just seckle yourself and take time out. It seems like you and drama is friend. Didn't I use to tell you: If you're arguing you're losing and if you've fought you've lost!

Yes, I understand your situation is crazy but there's a right and wrong way to do things. Emotionally you're unbalanced son. Whether you hit her or not is irrelevant. I never said that I thought you hit her. I said why did you do it? As in why did you go to her house? You should never been there in the first place. I saw the Instagram video so I don't wanna hear it.

I'm not judging you; you're my nephew and I love you. But I'm not gonna sugar coat nutin. Me and you ain't friend. You can't keep doing the same things and getting the same results. You can't. You can't. You can't bredrin. You can't keep letting people, as you young guys say, 'draw you out'. You can't keep blaming people for your actions. Because the only person that suffers is you. The only person losing time is you.

Aunty Jan Jan

Aunty Jan,

I didn't really wanna hear what you were saying in your letters.

But I've had time to think innit. And I know it's real talk what you're talking. But you don't understand. Those kids they mean everything to me. I don't have nothing else in the world but them. If I can't see them what's the point in having my freedom? Do you think I give a fuck about being on road if I can't see my own yutes?

I do have a lot of anger in me and this is where it comes from. The way I'm feeling right now Aunty, I feel to all blow up this girl's yard with me, her and my children in it. I know that's sounds like something Uncs would say, but that's how I feel. Aunty Jan, this shit is madding me.

D

Nephew,

I hear you again but I don't wanna hear them fool fool Taliban talk again. You better stop with all that chupid crazy talk 'bout blowing up people's house business. Get that shit outta ya mind, ya hear me?

How many times have I told you you can't always fight a battle by yourself? And when you know you're faced with certain situations where you're gonna make certain decisions, you can come to me and we can sit down and work it out. That's what I call family intervention, you handle things properly. You don't go around like some flipping mad man and cause more drama. Cos all you're doing is adding more fuel to the fire and that's how you're getting yourself drawn out. You're not focusing on the inner you.

OK, so you can't see the kids. Get yourself together from now so that when you finally get the chance to be with your kids, they can get to see a good man and a happy father. Not a man with anger inside. You don't want them to see all this drama. I know it's hard right now nephew, but try and have faith in the situation. And try praying. It will work itself out.

Aunty Jan Jan

Redz,

What's good my brudda?

Why you going on so stink about ATM. All I asked a man to do is look out for him. If you don't want to do it for him, it's bless, but I'm asking you to do something for me, init.

You know what, fam I've been doing a lot of thinking these last few days. Me and you have been bruddas from day one. My brother from another mother and all dat. We've never even had an argument. I tell a lie there was that one time in year 7 when you heard I was linking Simone from Clapton and you told me to stay away from her cos she's a Hackney gyal, remember that? LOL.

Anyway my G, we've been side by side on the front-line on some real Troy type of beef. We've seen mad paper together, got rushed together even beat couple chicks together LOL. The only thing that keeps man apart is jail-time, it's a fucking joke. The last time we was both on road at the same time man was 17. That's a good 7 years my G.

Not sure if you noticed it but times flying past us. And I don't know about you but I'm not the same 17 year old that you used to roll with. I've changed fam.

I shouldn't be in here this time. For once I'm innocent.

On some real talk Redz bro.

I read over your letters last night and I was thinking you don't really know what I'm on these days. And it kinda vexed me still. You wrote me some shit about the hoods got bare love for me and how everyone on the blocks rate me for not snitching. Cuz, d'you really think I give a fuck 'bout what the hood thinks of me? I'm gonna be 25 this month - what's the block ever done for us? Other than couple olders showing man about this trappin' ting, and schooling us on other negative bullshit.

The blocks got it confused cuz. Sometimes when I'm in my cell I just gotta laugh. Imagine I got this one brudder in here from North West who's forever watching me like I'm his gyal or sutt'n. I ain't got time to penny that though, I'm not trying to catch a m-charge.

On a level fam - what the fuck is a real nigga anyway? I ain't no slave. How can we be real men and real niggas at the same time? Man are so quick to go on Facebook and post pics about free my nigga this, free my nigga that, but I never got not one visit/letter and I don't see them trying to help me get my yutes back, but then they wanna say they're man's family? Worst still we're talking about freedom and using words like nigga. Are we really that lost?

I dunno about you Redz but I'm not tryna to be one of them 55 year old G's who jam under the garages all day reminiscing about the riots of '85. Imagine us man in 2030 drinking tenants reminiscing 'bout the riots of '2012 on a daily. That's dead.

Anyway enough of the hood talk. I'm just telling you this because you're my brother – blood in blood out. I just wanna make sure we're on the same page, cos the next time I lan' road, I'm not coming through Totty or H-town again, I'm done with the hood. The hood don't want man to grow up.

Nuff love my brudder, you always got mans back.

Bless king - I'll send you a VO soon. Peace!

Wha gwarn young G!

You bless?

Do me a favour bro, the second I land, I beg you remind me to buy
you a box of cotton buds. You YG's don't listen to shit. Feels like I'm
wasting my breath and my ink. Man aint got time to keep chatting to
you Young G's about your baitness. Which part of stay out of mans
passa didn't you hear? For the last time lickle brudda DO YOU, stop
involving yourself in my drama. I'm not on the roads no more!

I can't act like man weren't sitting in here grinning teeth when I
heard the ting got dropped. Cos I was. But when man heard why
the brudda had that change of heart I weren't smiling as hard.
I shouldn't be in here. Half the reason I'm still in the can is cos one
of my younger's was moving reckless. And you're there giving me
street ratings for keeping it real. What's real? Fuck real, real aint
really doing shit for me right now. And us man aint keeping it real
with you. On a level G, look around you, we don't even keep it real
between us on the block. If I was 'keeping it real' with man I woulda
never put a younger on to the game. I knew trappin was a trap. But
I didn't care; I was a two-time convict with new born twins darg.
You don't owe me shit, trust me darg. If anything I owe you. You was
a good kid with a bright future. I shouldn't have let it happen.

When I got put on remand man was vex with you. Trust me. I was
screwing sitting in my cell thinking why did this yute bait up my
whip after I told him not to touch it? Why don't this yute come
forward and own up to that shit. But then after a while I realised I
can't be mad with you. Cos it wasn't you that made me go to my
baby muddas that day, it was me. Seriously though, don't make it be
that I'm in here riding bird for you to find out you're coming here
to join me too. Or even worse still don't make me hear you got lick
down – touch wood.

Just the other day I was on the landing when one brudda bucked
me and asked me if I knew you. The brudda was easy, he just said
"You see your boy ATM?! Nuff big man in Belmarsh are looking
to do him sutin when they land road." Cos he's yanked up a man's

little brother or cos he bussed the ting outside a man's christening. I know you aint shook to do your ting. But you need to 'llow the hype ting G cah now you got a bag a man wanting to lick your head off.

Ain't you supposed to be a Dad right about now? Don't you wanna watch your yute grow ?

Duane

P.S. How come you ain't told me nothin 'bout the yute yet? You haven't even told me whether it's a boy or a girl?

Anyway, roll easy and hit me up when you can.

Mama Can't Raise No Man

Fam,

You know what, on some real shit I'm fed up of all your whinging.

That's all I see when I read your letters. I'm glad you're done with the preaching cos aint no one got time for that. And you're right about one thing, I don't owe you shit, man was just outchea tryna to hold it down for you and your namesake. For the last month I've been the one on the block daily having to hot up my own mandem when they're saying: Ricketts is a pussy!

I know you're not on the roads no more – I hear dat. But hear what I'm saying: I am innit! And everyone else who's still outchea doing this ting on roads knows I'm your younger. Those who don't like you don't like me. So what the fuck makes you think just cos you decide to change your life around and ignore your beef that the beef's gonna go away? Man on road who hated you hate me. So, any funny behaviour and mans getting it poppin.

Before man forget - stop sending bad-mind pussy'ole Redz to give me messages. I don't trust him and he's always been a Red-eyed cockblocker! If he weren't your bredrin trust me, man would have touched him time ago. Now I'm hearing this dick'eds a gang intervention officer – whatever the fuck that is.

Anyway, from today on I'm doing me! Don't chat to me until you get your balls back.

You kept asking me when my yute drops. My yute's dropped already darg, I had a little girl. We named her Angel cos she died at birth.

ATM

Anton,

You know what bruv, I'm gonna 'llow you this one time. I'm gonna hold my tongue because you got bigger things going on in your life right now.

It might surprise you but I know how it feels. I've never told anyone this before but me and Candy lost our first child too. I feel your pain my brother and I wish I could take it away. I wish I could bring your Angel back. Sometimes fucked up things in life happen which are out of our control. Life's not fair my brother.

Every man has his trials and tribulations. Every man has to carry his own cross. But you keep walking stong my brother. You know you're a solider already. I know your cross has been heavy from day one and that's why I've always tried to guide you.

Wherever your Angel is, just know she's not here for a reason greater than we'll ever understand. There's so much more I'd like to say to you but you know man ain't really on that sentimental ting.

Just make sure your missus is cool.

Keep your head up lickle brudder.

Duane

Son,

I have to be honest with you.

At first I was shocked and disappointed to hear that you were back in prison. But the truth is I'm not surprised at all.

Ah mi help you to be where you are. Ah mi pick your farder and brought you forth. And then I 'm gonna slam you telling you you're just like your father; well, what the hell should I expect? That is my major failure and for that I apologise. For my part in you being where you are, I apologise. I take full responsibility for being PART of the reason you're always in and out of prison.

One thing I can say me and you have in common Duane, is the stubbornness. I can't believe you still don't wanna talk to me. It's fine son I get that you're your own man now, but don't disrespect me and ignore me boy. Have some manners to write me or phone me and tell me you're still not talking to me.

I shouldn't have to find out through other people how my son is doing. I hope you're not still vex with me for kicking you out. But if you're are still vex at least come and talk to me about it. Be a man about yours, I'm still your mum and I know I raised you better than this.

Love you son – stay safe and pray!

And Happy Birthday for next week.

Mum

Mum,

I accept your apology.

But I don't see it the way you do. If I'd listened to you when I was growing up Mum I'm sure I wouldn't be doing this sentence right now. You ain't to blame.

I'm sorry too.

I'm sorry for all the times the yard got raided. I'm sorry for having you up in court and the judge looking down on you like you're a bad mum. I'm sorry that I've shamed the family with all this negative attention.

We need to sit down and talk properly, but while I'm in here, I still don't want no communication. I got too much going on to face that right now while I'm in here. I'm not trying to mad myself. I'd rather just wait till I'm on the outside to fix this.

I know this might sound really random but I need to contact my Dad. I've been thinking about it for some time now and my mind is made up. Can you give me some form of contact details for him? You always told me growing up if I wanted to contact him you knew where to find him. Well now I'm ready to make contact. I need answers.

Please don't feel no way because I wanna write to him and not you. But there's just something missing, I need to speak to this guy. I can't chat to you about certain things; I just need to have that man-to-man with this guy. I can't find peace until I do.

Duane

Bruv,

How you keeping? I got a bit of good news for once.

I know exactly where Candy and the kids are living. I found out from one girl who went school with me. Imagine I was in the Tesco on Seven Sister's Rd when some random girl shouted out my name and gave me a hug.

I didn't even know the girl bruv but she said she went Gladesmore with us. So I just smiled and acted like I remembered her. She started going on about school days - then hear her to me: "Your brother's kids are getting really big now innit!". Then she said how she sees them every day, and how they live a couple of doors away from her. Anyway the address I got for them is: 648 Middleton Road E8 Hackney.

At least now you know you can write the kids direct. I just hope Candy can put her emotions aside and let them read it and hopefully write you back. I know Candy's vex with you but I also know she's got a heart in there somewhere.

And it was really good coming to visit you the other day for your birthday. Big 25! Time's really flying bruv. You gave me too much joke. And you didn't need to give that boy that look for staring at me. Cos that's just what you guys do. You're all thirsty! Oh yeah and who was that guy staring you down, do you have beef with him or something?

I see Mum yesterday and she told me you finally wrote her back. I don't know what you said to her but she seems a lot less stressed.

Anyway bro good luck trying to get through to the kids. Love you D.

Rissa x

Look Candy,

I know you don't wanna talk to me right about now, let alone read my letters. I get that, I understand why you feel that way. I can only imagine how much I hurt you. What else can I say, man fuck'd up innit. All I can do is apologise for my past actions.

I know you say it's excuses but man didn't know the meaning of love. And I'm sorry for having to learn love lessons on your time. But one thing I do love are those kids. And those kids aren't just yours, they belong to BOTH of us. I never thought you would take a part of what I am. You've changed Candice, you know that! This ain't like you. Don't let your sister fool up your head with fuckery.

Remember what you said before Justice and Imarni were born. You said your Dad was a poor excuse of a man when he walked out on you and your mum when they broke up. You said if you ever broke up with the father of your child you would expect him to come and check for his children. You said you could never be one of them bitter baby-mother's who gets in the way of a man raising his child.

You said: "Any woman who stops a father from seeing their child is just wicked and badmind?" You said that.

The only way you could see yourself going to that extreme is if the father was some type-ah risk to your kids, or a women-beater. 'Member when you was chatting saying that any woman who does that for no good reason is a straight up bitch. That she can't truly love her kids if she does that. So does this mean you don't love yours?

Look at where we are. We don't need to be here.

Real talk Candy. You know I take good care of the kids. I dunno what's gotten into your head. I hope you know you're hurting the kids just as much as me, if not more. Enough is enough I'm not taking no talk. When I touch road I wanna see my kids.

Ain't it bad enough I'm in prison again? I know you don't care no more but if you knew half the pain I'm going through right now you would cut out the fuckery. I've lost mad weight since you've stopped me from seeing my yutes. You don't have to punish me no more. It's been mental enough already.

All I can ask is if you've read this, lets just put any bad vibes to one side and focus on what the kids want.

Just let my kids write me.

Duane

Wasteman,

Why am I coming to my sister's house seeing a prison letter by the door?

Bruv don't you get it? My sister don't want you no more. We all know you don't care about the kids, so stop acting up like you give some type of fuck.

You're too much of a fucking liard. You're right about one thing. It was me who told her to stop you from seeing the kids. Cos you're a wasteman.

You decided to walk out on your kids for how many months and now you wanna make out like my sister stopped you from seeing them. You gave up your fatherly rights when you walked out on them.

We don't need no man in our lives. The kids are good without you, they don't need no Dad. Especially one like you. You're just like all my baby fathers and we don't need any of you.

Lorna

Candy,

I don't know if you're gonna get this letter or your anti-man sister Lorna is gonna get it.

Lorna if you get this letter you need to learn to mind your own fucking business! Ever since I met Candy you've been butting your big forehead in our business. You need to learn to keep your nose and your forehead out of people's problems. You don't know shit 'bout what's gone on between me and your sister.

Candy if you open this letter I don't wanna argue with you either. I don't want beef. I wrote you before this but your sister got the letter and threw it in the bin. And I can't remember everything I said in that letter. But basically I wanna speak to my kids. Or at least be able to write them. So can you give me a landline number that I can call to speak to them on please? Or could you please get them to write to me. I need to speak to them.

I'm not giving up on what's mine and they both need a Dad and I need them. I'm sorry that I slept out on you. I was slipping and real men's feet don't slip. I knew better but I didn't do better, so I apologise for that. But let me be a good man to my kids at least.

P.S. If you get this letter Candy turn over the page and and give the letter to my kids please. I ran out of paper to write to them. Can you help them read it please?

[Attached letter]

Hey Justice and Imarni,

It's Daddy, I know you guys haven't seen Daddy in a while but sometimes in life things happen which are out of Daddy's control. Daddy is on holiday at the moment but when I come back I'm gonna take you guys to the park like I promised to do the last time I saw you. And we can get Ice-cream, sweets and all the stuff I say is bad for your teeth, we can get it all OK! I miss you guys so much. Justice my little Princess can you write me a letter and draw Daddy a picture please? I want to see your beautiful drawings while I'm on holiday. And Imarni Daddy's little soldier, can you write Daddy and tell me how your football match was? I'm sorry Daddy couldn't be there for your first game, but I didn't forget it, I hope you did your best and had fun playing.

Yo mi favourite nephew,

What the rarse is going on bredrin? I was on Tottenham High Road outside the bookies when I did see Rissa walking by with the baby. I'm there grinning teeth like some fool with her cos I just won a little £300 on one of the horse dem. Then I asked Rissa where you deh? And she tell me say you garn back a prison. And how you've been in there for a few months now. What type of fuckery is that. No one never tell me a rarse-ting dred.

Rissa done told me about the newspaper fuckery too. You see how they stay though. That's why I can't stand dutty Babylon. Dem never need fi put yuh photo in the newspaper front-page. Like say you're some wicked serial somebody. But don't mind Babylon mi nephew. Uncle Leroy knows you better than them, you're a good man with good intentions. No one can tell me no different.

I had to use the pen from the bookies and write you straight away dred. I was so vex to hear the fuckery. Your mudder and Aunty Jan deal with me wicked man. Dem never even bother call me and tell me wha gwarn. They never tell me a ting bredrin. You know what? I feel say they don't rate me again, you know. They're my sisters and I love em to bits, but this nephew is why I stop chatting to them from the millennium kick in. Vex I'm vex, only if you knew.

I don't wanna be writing you bad talking about my big sister dem cos you know I luv them bad even with all their ways. So done that talk, that's my argument wid them not yours. I hear say you're not talking to your mother again neph. Hear me good Rasta. You see your mother, that there is your Queen bredrin. And as long as she's breathing you have to try and honour her. Cah dat ah your Queen and you are the Prince bredrin. Enjoy her reign as Queen my nephew cos when she's gone bredrin truss me, you're gonna wish you wasn't the King so soon. Trust me. I miss my Queen bad.

But mummy aside - I'm vex with you king. What is it now; don't you rate your Uncle Leroy no more? I can't see you again! Bredrin, last time you come round by my yard it was all 2007 tu-rarse. And I remember cos it's when FIFA did first come out. I remember I did give you a 4-1 beating on the new FIFA. Since that beating you went missing on me dread. Serious though nephew, you cool? Why you never come to me for a lickle advice before you decide to go down to the girls' yard bredrin? I would of tell you straight - don't go there dred! You know I'm experienced in dealing with dem bad mind baby mudder business. Member dred, my first baby mudder, Pam, took 'way my eldest daughter when you was bout 2. Then my 2nd baby mudder, Monica, took 'way my boy and me daughter when you were bout 10. And you see how that one deh mash me up bad. I've been there Neph, I've worn your shoes. Mi know how yuh feel. Just know say you're not alone Nephew trust me. If you wanna get certain tings off ah your chest shout your uncle Lee. Don't hold the hurt in bredrin, cah that's what send nuff man ah mad house.

Nuff man what mi know have had their kids taken from them, it's f up still, it's not righted dred, but it's not just you one. Me all know a man whose wife leff him. She got the kids, she got the house, and he had to pay the mortgage for the yard bredrin. And to top it off bredrin the uman's got her new man living up in that same yard with her and her pickney dred. The systems not nice bredrin, nuff fuckery ah gwarn for man in general.

Anyhow Dred, don't go on like you're too big to write me back. I'm gonna drink a quick two white rum, finish my ital spliff and find me bed.

Respect general. Keep the faith.

Uncle Leeroy

Wha gwarn Uncs? You good?

You give me joke every time Uncs. I could tell you was slightly
wavey by the way you wrote me that letter. Whenever you swear
and write me in an accent I know you've been hitting that white
Rum with your best friend Wray and his Nephew. LOL.

Yeah, I'm back in the shithole again Uncs, I fucked up man. 3 and a
half years. So I'll do about half and hopefully get put on tag after
that. Of course I'm pissed right now, mostly cos I can't get to see
my yutes, but I don't even wanna talk on it.

And no disrespect to you Uncs but the last time I think I came to
you for advice I must have been about 9. I know you've been there
for me in other ways before but I'm a man who does my own thing.
It's mad cos if I was able to go back to last month before I lost it. It
might have made more sense to just to pick up my phone and call
you instead of going there. But everything happens for a reason.

You gimmie joke though why do you expect Aunty Jan and Mum
to call you and tell you family stuff, like me being in here? I swear
it was you who stopped talking to them in 2000? LOL. That's like
8 years Uncs. Come on man, it don't make sense you being vex
about it. Just remember Aunty Jan and Mum are just as stubborn as
you. They rate you highly don't ever get it twisted. They just don't
respect what you're doing to yourself. They're disappointed to see
you going off the rails with all the drink, smoking and gambling.
Maybe you should slow it down a bit now Uncs. You aint getting any
younger. I know it's hard out 'ere but that won't really help.

Nuff love for the letter Uncs... Get at me next time when you're
sober.

Duane

P.S. Uncs what are you on these days; about the last time you saw
me was when you beat me at FIFA? Uncs you ain't never beat me!
You better 'llow the drinking for real cos that shit's playing with
your brain cells. Since you're a betting man, put your money where

your mouth is. When I lan' road, I'll play you again. You can pick any team you like. You can pick Barca and I'll pick one of dem dead lower league teams like Watford and I'll still give you a brushing. About you beat me LOL Mad-Man.

PHONE CALL: DUANE TO MARRISA

DUANE
Wha gwarn Riss? Quickly Gimme a landline
number I can call you back on.

MARRISA
0208-932-0203 but can you cal...

HANG UP TONE

**DUANE CALL'S BACK. PHONE RINGS. MARRISA OUT
OF BREATH AS SHE ANSWERS**

MARRISA
Hello.

DUANE
How you taking so long to answer the
phone when I just said I'm gonna call
you back?

MARRISA
You're such a doughnut I was downstairs
bringing up the shopping. If you weren't
so fast to hang up you would've have heard
me trying to tell you that.

DUANE
I know, I know but these prison phones
keep dunning my credit. Anyway what's good?
You spoke to Mum? She's meant to be doing me
a favour but she's on some long ting.

MARRISA
Yeah I spoke to Mum. Why the hell would
you wanna make contact with him? What's he
ever done for you? He ain't
ever did shit for us. So why now?

DUANE
I know.

MARRISA
He's not once tried to make contact
with us, so why you tryna make
contact with him?

DUANE
I know sis. I didn't expect you to
understand.
That's why I didn't tell you. I was
gonna tell you after I made contact with
him and heard what he's got to say
for himself. But obviously Mum couldn't
hold it down.

MARRISA
Mum didn't tell me directly. I came
into her house last week and used my
spare key cos Destiny needed to use the
toilet. Then I overheard her shouting on
the phone saying: ''I can never forgive
you for leaving me to raise two children
alone''

DUANE
Is it.. Like that

MARRISSA
Yeah, Mum cussed him out then when I came
in the room she hung up the phone.

DUANE
Did she get an address?

MARRISSA
No, Don't think she did. But he's
got yours.

                    DUANE
                 That's cool.

                   MARISSA
          So what you gonna say to Dad
              when he writes you?

                    DUANE
          Sis my credits 'bout to done. Don't
          forget to send me the letter.

                   MARRISSA
          Don't try it, your credit ain't...

HANG UP TONE

**MARRISSA: Kisses teeth. Laughs and mumbles to
herself "Ginnal!"**

Yo my dargy,

Wha gwarn? You went ghost on a brother. I hope you aint still 'llowing man to violate the ting!

Man's just out 'ere tryna 'get it in' that legit paper. A lot's been going on for me out 'ere. And we aint spoke for a hot minute. So Imma fill you in with the latest. I've been moving differently out here. You know like what you were doing; just keeping my head low trying to apply myself. I even got a job fam. Who would of thought, a man like me getting a job? Especially with my rap record – NO Qualifications –NO work experience, nothing! 25 years of my life and I didn't have a thing to put on my CV - except for my personal profile interest and hobbies. LOL.

FAM, when I bought in my CRB and handed it to the manager he looked up at me from the top of his glasses. He took copies and had to put it in a folder bruv. Cos that shit weren't fitting in no paper sleeve like the others he had laying on his desk. But it's all good cos mans working, I'm a suit and tie man now.

I've been hearing bare man are getting taken off road in the hood though. They did couple raids all over Totty the other day. It must be clean up season. Your younger soon join them. I'm still out 'ere hearing his name. He must of moved to one the olders the other day. You 'member Ziggy from near Ida? Anyway he was jamming on the farm and your boy ATM was meant to be saying he was a snitch, then he gun-butt him and bussed two shot by his foot and chased him out of the block. My yute thinks he's in some cowboy movie bruv.

I know that's your younger but I caught him screwing me in Peppers and Spice on the High Road when I was on my lunch break. You better chat to him cos if he tries to violate me I'm really gonna fuck him up.

Other then all that shit, it's all good out here. Don't forget anything you need I got you my brother. Have you wrote to Keisha yet? Lemme know if you want some jezzies to write to. I gave out your address to couple grim tings that use to write me when I was in there. So expect the unexpected soon. LOL

And don't stress a thing about P's. I'm trying to make a good impression at my job so if I do when you touch road, I might be able to get a brother a job.

Stay up my Darg

Different way of living but still M.O.E (Money over Everything...)

Redz

Duane,

I got a knock on my door from your Mum the other day. She told me you was looking for me. Sorry you're only hearing from me now I'm not the easiest person to get a hold of. But when Audrey said you needed answers I knew what I had to do.

I really don't know what to say Duane, well not after 25 years. So I'll just introduce myself and we can start from there.

Hello son, my name is Errol Thompson, that's right it's me your

Dad.

Wha gwarn Errol?

What's good? It's your boy Duane you 'member me?

I felt I had to shout you real quick. Like...

Where the fuck you been darg? Where you been hiding? 21 fucking years you've been ghost and to add shame to that I had to contact you first! Don't you feel some kinna way about that? What kinda man does that bruv? I mean you just ducked out on man at age 4! Why did you let me grow without you? You left me to figure out this manhood journey thing on my jacks. Nigga you never taught me shit, not to fight, ride a bike, fix a puncture, none of that sort of shit. You left my Mum to try raise me by herself. Mum taught me how to box. Mum raised me up alone on the block. And that ain't half of it bredrin. It gets embarrasin', Mum taught me from young how a man must wash his cock. You're a bitch nigga bro you left me out to dry. I never saw you nowhere, not even a little parents evening, nothing! You were missing bruv. You didn't leave us with shit, further more you aint shit.

You left Mum to carry the extra weight.

You didn't make me over-stand manhood or what life might have in store for me. Instead you left me to figure this shit out on my own! Sometimes I thought "maybe if my Dad stayed around I wouldn't have made as much mistakes as I did!" I had to learn manhood the hard way bredrin.

Where was you when Mum was working her ass off for chump change trying to put food on the table and clothes on me and my sister? I learnt from young I had to step up quick and be the man you was suppose to be. I felt I had to wear the trousers and do your job. To protect and provide for my family, like I learned a man should. But the problem was I wasn't ready to be the man of the house, I couldn't get your trousers to fit bruv. I spent so much time trying to wear your trousers and get them to stay on that when I tried putting my own pair back on I found myself in problems. So in the end I said fuck it and started wearing shorts, and kept coming up short. Ya get me Old G.

Hear what I'm saying though Errol, if you decide to write me again that's fine but don't make the mistake of referring to me as son again. You ain't no Dad to me, you're just Errol.

I'm not writing you to play happy families I just want some answers.

Duane

Note for Candice:

(Please let my kids read this letter. Thank you for letting them read the last one and for letting them write back to me too – it's appreciated. Attached are 2 separate letters, one for Imarni and one for Justice. P.S. I've sent some stamps and envelopes, so you don't have to go out of your way to do that again. Thanks for meeting me halfway)

Hi Justice,

How are you doing baby-girl? You Ok? Daddy's been missing you guys man. But I don't worry about you cos Daddy knows you're a big girl now and I know you're very smart too. Smart enough to know that Daddy isn't a naughty boy and he shouldn't be in prison. You are right, somebody did a very BIG mistake, (You make Daddy laugh baby-girl).

I wanna tell you something Justice. The other day Daddy was sitting in this stinky boring place they call jail. And I was being very miserable. You know like when you got your grumpy face on and Daddy tells you to fix your face? Well I had that exact same grumpy look. But then something magical happened I got a letter from you and saw the lovely picture you drew. And my miserable face disappeared. I had the biggest smile on my face and I started to feel much better.

I need you to promise Daddy something. Promise me that no matter what bad things happen in life that you will stay strong and keep smiling... Can you promise me that Princess?

And don't worry about Imarni, I promise you he will never come to jail. Don't ever talk like that hunny. Don't even think like that – you hear me? Just enjoy being a child and leave Daddy to handle Imarni OK.

You make Daddy so proud. I liked the way you drew the family, me, your Mum, your brother and the other lady. It was lovely to see all of us together in the house. You drew the sky and the sun really well too. And I liked the way you drew the garbage man throwing out the rubbish. I liked all of it. One question who is the other lady in the house standing between me and your Mummy? Is that Nana June?

Anyway baby I hope you're trying your hardest at school. I love you loads and loads never you forget that Miss Justice Ricketts.
Speak soon xxx

Hi Son,

What's going on? I've been worried about you. And so is your sister.

I'm hearing you've been getting yourself into fights at school. What's wrong Imarni? Is someone troubling you at school? I've never known you to ever get yourself into fights before. I'm so sorry that I can't be by your side while all this is going on. So I need you to write me – OK? I may not be by your side physically but I'm here anytime you need me.

Anytime, all you have to do is write me and imagine you're talking to me. And do me a favour try your best to be a good boy for Mummy because you don't want to be standing at the wall anymore - do you? That's boring son, that's what I do every day. Don't think that Mummy doesn't love you because she shouts at you, it's just Mummy's way of trying to make you stay a good boy while Daddy's away.

I got the feeling you didn't write back to me cos you're angry with me. But I hope you're not angry, Daddy didn't mean for this to happen. I'm so sorry for being in jail and I'm sorry for letting you down. But when I come back I'm gonna make it up to you son. I promise you. We can go and watch a live football match in the stadium. I'll take you to watch Arsenal play OK? Love you to bits son. You're the best son a Dad could ask for. You're the best son in the world.
Hope to see a letter from you Imarni.

Be a Good boy Mr Ricketts. (love you son)

Duane,

I've read your letter now.

What can I say? I never knew you were so angry with me. Don't get me wrong, I expected you to be angry but I never knew the anger ran so deep inside you.

I never knew me not being there for you hurt you so much. But now it's clear to see the damage caused. I hurt you bad, son, didn't I?!

Listen Duane, you got every right to be mad at me - every right. But in your letter you asked me how could I not stay and teach you how to be a man. And the truth is some questions don't have the answers we want to hear. I can't promise to have all the answers but if you could just calm down a bit and ask me what it is you want to ask me then I will try my best to be a man about it and answer your questions properly. I don't want to have no more excuses.

Dad

Man like Errol! Wha gwarn?

Quick-question: Did you even read my letter?

Nah. I don't think you did, you must of skim read that shit. I beg you go pick it up and read it again.

Listen Errol; let's get one thing straight, I'm not feeling all this son talk. I ain't got a Dad. You're just the man who breeded my Mum.- so dead that son talk you hear what I'm saying? It's funny how you remember the word son now. The same son you didn't know fuck all about for the last two decades. Where the fuck was you when man needed to be called son?

Furthermore, have I got any siblings out there I don't know about? I bet I have. I bet I got a bag of brudders and sisters running round town from you.

Have you ever just sat down and checked yourself? I could've been dead all these years. Real talk and would you even have known about it? What... what was it gonna take for you to turn up – my funeral? Man could of been dead on the roads and what would you have done? Try come talk to my gravestone after like: "Oh I'm sorry son!" Fuck you! You did me a wrongen bruv and you still ain't saying shit.

Another question - after 25 years, what the fuck d'you mean you never knew your absence could have caused us or me so much damage? So what, what did you really think was gonna happen when you bounced? Did you think my Mum was gonna have it easy? Don't go on like you ain't heard the saying: "Mama Can't Raise No Man!"

Further more, you're there chatting shit, saying you didn't know this, you didn't know that but all now I haven't even got an apology from you. Not one little sorry. Right about now you should be on your knees rude-bwoy. Saying "I'm sorry Duane, I'm sorry... can you ever forgive me? I know I fucked up". Everything should be I'm sorry – ya get me!

Oh, and another question, was you on drugs back then? Cause I don't understand it —what made you just walk away? And not turn back, why didn't you look back? Like say we didn't matter! Don't think I could ever be like you bruv. My Mum taught me better. She taught me that the only time a man's meant to turn his back on his child is when he's giving them a piggy back.

You know what, to tell you the truth I'm fucking ashamed to be your son. I'm pissed to look in the mirror and know I came from you. How about that? I know I'm far from perfect but at least I ain't like you.

I've been through a whole load of shit. Not saying you haven't cos I don't know shit about your life. But unlike you I didn't bitch out and run. I keep fighting for mine. Ya get me, and I will never turn my back on my kids no matter what. Rich or Poor. Ya feel me, no matter what! You know what bruv don't feel say you have to write me back after this letter. Cos... what's the point? What can you... What is it that you can... you can't fucking chat to me. It's too late. I'm already a man!

Duane

Duane,

I'm tired of beating around the bush, you want the truth? Truth is I wasn't ready to have you. You weren't part of my plan. I'm sure you've been there yourself. I thought I was a man back then. I thought I knew what I was doing when I met your mum, but clearly I didn't.

You wanna know why I walked out; OK, I just hope you're ready. I remember the last time I saw you clearly.

The last time I saw you it was your 4th Birthday. We was in Toys R Us and I was buying a bike for my son. I remember you always had plenty energy and loved ramping with your sister. You got so excited ramping that you tripped spun round full circle and landed on your back. When I leaned over to pick you up your Mum gave me the wickedest look I've ever seen, and told me to back off.

Sounds a bit harsh innit? But I can't wrong your Mum. You see Duane when I said I was buying a bike for my son, I wasn't talking about you. You were right you do have another brother and sister, but they were in the picture before you were. And that day in Toys R Us I just happened to bump into you and your Mum when I was with them. And my whole world blew up in my face. I hope you get what I'm trying to say here.

Your Mum was my side-chick.

I thought I loved your Mum, but I didn't. I did actually care for her. I had plenty of love for her, she was a good woman. What she didn't know was that I was married and had two young kids with another woman before I met her.

Anyway, after a while of cheating on my woman with your Mum, things started to get better at home. I wanted to fix up and I realised my wife and kids were worth fixing up for. So I went to break it off with your Mum for good.

And that's when she dropped the news that she was 3 months

pregnant with you. I was pissed. I didn't wanna give my woman that hurt and shame. So I bitched out, I turned to your Mum and told her to get rid of you.

Your Mum just gave me one look and said: "Errol, you got a nerve, you aint shit! I can do this by myself." She was well vex. She cried until her face was covered in mascara. I'm not proud of it son. Then she stopped crying and said she's keeping you with or without me.

So I stayed, I stayed to see you come into this world. Did you matter? Of course you did, but like I said I had a family before you were born. For whatever it's worth, I took you to the park, I tried to teach you how to kick-ball. I watched you speak your first words - which so happened to be Da-da. Most of this you probably don't even remember, but you can always ask your Mum.

By the time you turned 2 I realised the double life wasn't a life I could live. So one evening I tried to man-up and said: "Look Audrey we need to talk." Before I got to open my mouth and talk she said: "Yes! We do need to talk Errol I'm pregnant again." At that point I was more desperate to jump ship than ever. I just said the same thing to her as I did with you. "Audrey you have to get rid of it I don't want another child with you."

Your Mum just gave me that same cut-eye again this time without the tears but I could still see the hurt. This time when she said she's keeping your sister with or without me I just zipped up my jacket, walked through the front door and said without.

I fucked up son. I bitched out; I was scared of losing my family. And I wasn't man enough to take care of my responsibilities. You and your sister. I should've been there to read to you, take you to the park, kick ball with you, parents evening, support you financially, all of that stuff. But I wasn't.

You're a bigger man than me Duane; it takes courage to contact the man who walked out on you 21 years ago. I respect that you want some answers and not a relationship. So I have to ask myself, how the hell can I deny you that after what I've done?

We don't have to be friends, but you can ask me whatever you want. I just hope my truth doesn't hurt you too much. Take care Duane.

Errol

PHONE CALL: DUANE TO MARRISSA

DUANE
Yo Riss whats going on — you
good?

MARISSA
Yeah bro I'm ok just cooking a little
food for me and Destiny. How you been I
ain't heard from you in about a month.

DUANE
I'm just 'ere innit. How's my favourite
niece doing?

MARRISSA

LAUGHING

You mean your only niece, and she's
doing just fine.

DUANE
Good that's what I like to hear. Anyway
I've moved prison - Swaleside.
They shipped me out two weeks ago. Me and a
few others including that same bredda you saw
screwing me on the visit.

MARRISSA
Is there beef between you? Where do you know
him from?

DUANE
I don't know the bredda and I don't give a
fuck about what his problem is. Anyway is
everything good with you?

MARRISSA
I'm good, don't worry about me. Are you good
though? Do you need anything?

Cos if you do I think Redz posted some
money for you through the door again
yesterday.

DUANE
Wicked, I love Redz for that. One of the
realist brothers I know.

MARISSA
On the note of brothers have you heard
about your younger bro ATM?

DUANE
Nah, what now.

MARISSA
Not to talk too much but there was a
shootout at the all dayer in farm
and everyone's calling up your boy's name.

DUANE
What...? I tried to tell
him there's a difference between being a
man on road and being a man in real life.
But he weren't hearing shit. I'm done talking
to him now.

MARISSA
I hear what you're saying bruv but ATM
acts humble around you, he rates you
highly. You're like a God to him.

DUANE
Nah sis he rates my old lifestyle. The
wild me that had paper. The yutes lost.

MARRISSA
I didn't even know you lot weren't
talking regular. I saw him the other day at

McDonald's in front of me in the queue.
Without asking me he bought Destiny a
Happy Meal and ice cream. The boy's cool
man. He just wants to be like you. Maybe
he is lost but maybe you can be the one
who helps him find himself?

DUANE
The yute gets too disrespectful,
I try but I can't deal with that. I'm not
Neo and this aint the matrix. He has to save
himself sis.

MARRISSA
Anyway you spoke to that man yet?

DUANE
Which man?

MARRISSA
You're Dad!

DUANE
LAUGHING
Our dad. Yeah we made contact
It's long getting into it but he's
just chatting bare shit. Bare excuses.
Anyway don't give it out my
address to no one
unless you ask me first. Only people
who had the last one and not Mum.

MARISSA
Cool.

DUANE
Write me when you can.

MARISSA
Cool bro take care.

DUANE
Love sis.

Wha gwarn Redz my brudder!

Just wanted to show some appreciation for the love you've been showing. My sis told me you've been dropping P's through her door for me. Good looking out for that my G, you know how pissed a man is when he's in jail and he aint got no-one sending him money in here. But yeah differently though I have been missing for a bit. Just trying to keep ma head down ya feel me. And I got shipped out of Pents couple weeks ago, so man's up in Swaleside now. Weren't you in here before?

Anyway why you giving all these jezzies my address? I got Keisha and Mon sending me naked pictures and shit. And chatting bout what they wanna do to a brother when I land road. LOL. Leave me out cuzzy. I don't need my name getting caught up in anything to do with them gyal. Infact any gyal full stop bro. Right now fam I just wanna deal with this situation. No homo shit but beg you don't give any old links my prison details.

And 'llow me with all this am I getting violated shit. You out of all people know what I'm like when I lose it. When that switch goes I don't fear no man but God. So lord knows we can get it on. Funny enough I think I see couple of them North West boys that we had beef with back in the dayz when we was in Feltham - remember them yutes we had to bruck up on A-wing? You know when they tried to buss open your cell door and move to you that time over that pool table incident?

Well them yutes anyway. There's couple other North man in here with me and I'm sharing a cell with one bait Hackney yute. But he's cool anyway. He don't care about that Hackney and Tottenham bull-shit. So just the same old shit. I see couple other yute man I got into it with from back in the day giving me screw face. But that's cool, man can screw face me all they want, that shit don't bother me. Screw face ain't hurting me. As long as they don't put their hands on me we're bless. Anyway man's gonna go hit the gym.

Before I forget - Big up yourself for getting that new job bro. Good to know the money your sending me isn't putting you at risk for recall. Man's over proud to hear you're working. Don't worry 'bout getting me a job bro just keep progressing in a positive way. MOE Money Over Everything – Legally now... Bless brudder.

Duane

Yo Duane wha gwarn?

I know we ain't been seeing eye to eye for the last few months. But thanks for your last letter I wasn't expecting a reply.

And you know I didn't mean it when I said you're moist. Come on fam how can I be calling you moist when you made me tough as a yute man. You taught me how to move with da ting so don't take my last letters of disrespect too seriously. You're the only older that never use to bully man coming up. And I've always looked up to you for that cos it's not like you weren't holding down the block before knocking out man who use to violate the ting.

I didn't mean half the things I said. I was just vex cos my yute died in my arms. I have to rate you for not switching at my disrespect. You could have turned your back on me and washed your hands of me but instead you felt a brother's pain and tried to understand where my head was at. To me that's real love. I know I forget myself sometimes but I rate the way you accept me for me and never give up on man. I know you've always got my best interest at heart but you've changed and I don't always understand where you're coming from.

You've changed. The Duane I remember, that man we use to call Trigger, was a real g. Man respected you from all over back in the day. And now look at you getting all positive and shit and living by this bullshit self defence mentality like your name's Karate Kid. But what about Money Over Everything? What happened to attack being the best form of defence? Man like you taught me how to live by that manhood code and now you're acting like a man who can't do his ting.

I know you're not a pussy but why are you letting next dogs bark at you? You taught me if anyone puts their hand on me, to break their hand. But you're in there letting man put their hand, knee and foot on you.

Anyway you don't have to chat to me after you read this cos I ain't changing for now. My yutes dead bills have gotta get paid and I ain't letting no man violate me while I'm outchea trapping. I know you probably hear chat that I'm going on reckless, but I'm not, I'm just not having it from no one. I got you for paper and anything else if you need just holla.

Also, Redz, he isn't who you think he is. The whole hood's been saying he's acting dodgy. I'm not trying to bad mind your homeboy cos he can actually be a really cool brudder but under that nice guy act, he just can't help being who he is. I know he's your code-D and this might be hard to hear. If you don't drop that rat out your circle he's gonna start chewing through your shape. No hard feelings.

Bless up big bro.

ATM

Wha gwarn mi favourite nephew?

It's been a couple of months bredrin. I see your Mum walk by with Rissa outside the bookies earlier today. I asked Rissa for you and she said how Babylon took you to a different human zoo, name Swaleside.

Anyhow I had to beg her for the address dred. She said you told her not to give it to no one and I had to mek her know seh my name ain't no one, it's Uncle Leroy. I said hello to your Mum and the woman just looked me up and down and blanked me. Vex I was vex bredrin.

Real talk mi nephew, you know I can't take embarrassment, facetiness or any form of fuckery. I had to ask her how she can still be carrying on so stink over the one lickle disagreement we had in year 2000! In fact you were there. We were at the dinner table; me, you, my two sister dem Jan and Audrey.

Your Mum and Jan started chatting some fuckery about men. I really can't remember what she said that rubbed me the wrong way. Some fuckery about women can adapt and men can't multi-task and women are stronger and more reliable than their partners. And how: "most single mothers like me have to be the mother and the father because some men ain't man enough to take care of their responsibilities."

I tried to hold my mouth and not speak my mind. Cos one thing I learnt growing up is that a woman's worse weapon is her mouth. That's why I could never win no arguments with my sisters growing up. But my good friends Wray and him Nephew told me to man up and say what's on my mind... So I did.

I stood up with my friends and said: "Unu need to cut out the fuckery! Stop put down the black man cos unu don't understand him. And stop fool up each other's head chatting about a woman can be a mother and father. Some women are great mothers but one hand can't clap tu-rarse.

Bredrin all 9 years later I don't know what made me farse up ma-self and be so direct. Then I got braver and added: "God never put woman on earth to father. If he did he would have made woman man instead of woman". I got bredrins who are single fathers, and not one of them would say they can teach their daughters how to become women, Nah dred she needs a woman for that.

Some woman love say, I can do it alone, but does that benefit the pickney! Boy or girl child!

I don't know what it's like to be no single mother. But I feel it for the ones forced to do it alone. Ah suh it go sometime. Right now this lickle white rum in my hand has got me emotional. I'm gonna go smoke two ganja to ease off the emotion and go out with Reggie and the boys to play two Domino.

Uncle Leeroy

Yo Bredrin!

I know I did write to you yesterday but me and the boys had a deep conversation about feminism at Reggie's yard while we played dominos last night. Certain times Reggie can talk a bag of shit but when he's ready him cyan chat a bit of sense too. Last night he was on one, and he did sound like one of them professor boys which come out of Oxford – but don't tell him I said that coz you know his head's swell up already.

But anyway, Reggie was saying something 'bout how a man will leave his house from early in the morning and take all the fuckry that Babylon has to offer and who is he doing that for? His family bredrin!

Then Reggie start one lecture talking 'bout when the Feminism Act came into play and how dem times a lot of da sistas bought into this feminist fuckery movement. He said how many of them didn't fully understand its agenda. He started chatting 'bout how you had the white woman fighting for economic equality and wanting to get get paid as much as their men were. Man-ah-man can't knock them for that cos that's fuckry. Farder-god knows if I was a woman, I would be pissed if a man was getting paid more just coz he's a man.

But Reg was saying how a lot of the sista's blindly bought into that feminism stuff. They never see that when a lot of these feminists were there chatting 'bout independence, and standing up for themselves, they weren't fighting for the black woman, they were chatting 'bout economic equality for the white woman.

But real talk neph, for our women to go and chase that form of change, it wasn't productive for us as a people cos we had something different going on. Something totally different. Our struggle at that time was about more than economic equality. We were still facing racism. Imagine going to rent a yard with your missus, bredrin, and the landlord wanna come with their 'No Blacks, No dogs, No Irish fuckry'! When you're confronted with that kind of rasicm, how can a black woman's fight for feminism be the same as a white woman's?

You know me already bredrin, I'm all up for girl power, freedom of rights and dem tings dere but after hearing Reggie chat, it made me look at how feminism played a part in dividing our community.

When you check it, Black men are not responsible for the negative position the sista's are in as a black women because we don't control this society or have equal standing within it. The black man is not being a barrier to her being treated as an equal in society. If a black man is doing negative things to hold his women back, it's usually out of ego or his own social construct of not being able to manoeuvre himself within a system set up against him. It's not from some big master plan to suppress her. Yuh hunderstand! So therefore any sista who was fighting for feminism was tarring the black man and the white man with the same brush. When these black men aint even in no good position in the first place.

Anyway neph, wanted to share the conversation with you real quick but. I gotta hurry and get my Wray and Neph now, all this sober talk is hurting my head bredrin.

Stay out of trouble and write me back

Bless up mi Lion — walk strong

Uncle Leeroy

Duane,

How you doing?

I heard the good news that you are back in contact with your children. That's fantastic news. I wrote you two letters within the last month with no response. So I went by Audrey's house during the week to find out how my big sis is keeping and what's going on with you. And as soon as I mentioned your name to her, she burst out crying. And you know your Mum don't cry easy.

She really misses you. I tried to confort her and remind her that you will be back home this time next year but it didn't help much. The thing she's finding hard to cope with isn't the amount of time, it's the fact that you're not talking to her.

Imagine how your Mum's feeling right now. I'm not here to play no guilt trip but you know how it feels when you can't see your child.

I know my sister aint easy, God knows. But you can't turn your back on your Mum, you can't live certain ways. Try not to be negative towards her because she is somewhat a reflection of you. Find the respect. If you have to love her from a distance, then do that. We're all going through things. She's no different cos she's your mum.

Don't reject her son. My sister never got a handbook on how to raise you.

Even when you don't hear from me just know I'm here for you whenever you need me. Don't feel like you're doing time alone. Write me back soon and stay out of harm's way. Bless xx

Aunty Jan-Jan

Bruv,

How you keeping?

Duane, not saying this cause you're my brother but from what I see of you, I think you're a proper good Dad.

But right now I need to tell you what's been going on before it drives me crazy. Jerome's been doing me and Destiny some kind of fuckery. You know we broke up like 2 years ago right? When we was together he was trying to be a good dad but he ain't seen her for well over a year now! My man just done an Errol and turned his back on her.

And now I'm left to pick up the pieces. You know what it's like for me to have to hear my daughter ask questions like: "Mummy why doesn't daddy love me no more?" That shit brings tears to my eyes. I got vex and phoned to cuss him out but when I called this girl answered and told me that she was Jerome's girlfriend, and that he lives with her and her five-year-old son. How is this fool looking after a next girl's child when he don't even take care of the one he's got? KMT.

He hasn't called back since. The way I feel bruv I shouldn't even let him even see Destiny no more. But feelings aside he's still her Dad. But it's breaking her heart and I don't know what to do anymore Duane. I beg u chat to this fool for me. Cos there's only so much I can do.

I feel like he's only doing this to Destiny cos I didn't wanna be with him no more. If he can't see her at my house he doesn't wanna take her. It's like he's using her as a weapon. I just don't get it. Me and Jerome both come from broken homes, like why would he want the next generation to go through what we had to?

Why can't he understand that every girl child needs her father. Especially when we hit secondary school, we need our Dads the most. I'm not saying a girl can't ask her mum for advice but when it comes to boys it's better coming from her Dad; well that's how

Mama Can't Raise No Man

I felt growing up anyway. Even myself I realise now that I needed a male role model around. Jerome needs to come back, Destiny needs him. I've seen it damage girls around me and even partly in myself and I don't want that for my daughter. I want her to feel loved by her Dad without having to question his love. He don't even phone her and he's supposed to be the first man she can trust. I can't believe he's just gone and dissed us like this after all of these years.

All I can tell Destiny everyday is: "You know what babe you know your Dad loves you innit!"

It's fucked how someone like me had to have an arsehole of a baby-father like Jerome. Then you get them messed up baby-mothers that take the piss out of the good fathers – y'nah wat I mean.

Sorry for sharing the extra drama. but I just needed to vent. Love you bro.

Marissa X

Riss,

I literally just read your letter. So, what you saying now? Jerome done a Usain Bolt on you and my niece?

You know what.... I don't even know why I'm acting all shocked. When I really check it I should know better. Not making any excuses for the yute but I can see why a brudder like Jerome could just bounce and leave his family. Why? Cos my man never had his family growing up. Look at Jerome's mum, look at his dad — both fenes.

I'm not trying to bring up old shit or throw anything in your face. But I was trying to tell you from day one sis. From you first brought him to Mum's living room and introduced us to him as your "So called friend." I told you and Mum I wasn't feeling him. I told you I didn't like that bait yute sitting in Mum's yard. Nothing personal, I just didn't like the fact that I knew Jerome's name before I even knew his face.

You weren't trying to hear it. Even Mummy had a soft spot for him when you told her that his parents were both drug addicts and he grew up in care. But truth be told I didn't care about his story my spirit didn't tek to him.

Fuck it I don't even know why I'm going into all of that I'm just vex to hear this sis. Like why the fuck didn't you tell me he bounced when I was on road? At least I could have spoke to him and told him to fix up look sharp...

You know what sis I'm so sorry. As a man and a big brother I'm so sorry he's done this to you. There ain't really much I can do from in here to get through to my man. But don't worry just try and hang tight for now. And when I land road next year me and my man will have words.

Keep your head up and remember 3 things. 1. You're a soldier. 2. You're not alone. And 3. I got your back
Duane X

Nephew,

You see the drinking ting? Listen to this now: Everybody wanna be BIG – Everybody wanna be SOMEBODY – Everybody wanna be a BIG SOMEBODY. Yuh understand? You see Me, I wanna be a NOBODY! You know why? Cos nobody knows nothing about a nobody.

I don't business y'nah Duane. When people ask me who I am, I say I'm a nobody, cos nobody knows iyah, nobody knows. You understand. Somebody tink dem know, but dem never noooo – nobody knows. Yeah...

Yuh understand, I wanna be a NOBODY, I don't care! Yeah I don't care! I don't care call me a drunky, I wanna be nobody. I don't wanna be somebody in dem silly sittin there. Cos nobody knows. When you're somebody Babylon wanna come kill yuh. Look how dem kill off Malcolm X, Dr King and dem man dere. Nah dred, I wanna be a nobody yuh understand.

You see the ting with me nephew, me nah inna no Hen-club. Hen club - you see, you see when you have too much hen together yuh understand, you have a Hen-Club. You see when I use to deal with my yute, from the yute born – Hen-Club. Mudda... Sista... Cousin... all just hens together, all women together. So when I try say boy hear what, I want my yute to be like this, or do tings a certain way. They would try get involved and start muddle cuddle him up, or deal wid him so. They don't listen! They just get in there Hen-Club together and carry on doing what they tink is right! Cos it's a Hen-Club yuh understand. Everywhere you go it's a hen club. Just pure Hens together, they don't want no cock inna the Hen-Club. Yuh understand, straight, ah just Hen-Club! So when I come to say hear what I want my boy to be raised like this and rare tear, ah pure war mi ah war with dem!

Brudda, one time now yuh understand. My 1st baby mudder tek the yute dem. Take the yutes dread. I was like rah where's my yute? All two weeks, I don't see the yute. Kmt. Brudda I got drunk one time, nobody didn't answer the phone so I kick off the front door. I said me kick off the front door and go inna dere. Sit down and wait. All 5 days later they come. The police get called, all dem type of ting dere cos I kick off the door. My baby mudders mum said to me boy 'ere what she wouldn't mind if I did dead. I'm the farder of her Grandchild! And she tell me say she wouldn't mind if I did dead – kmt. That ah true story by the way. LOL. Yuh understand?

You see dem kinna disrespect man affi go under? Yuh understand, so rarseclart its better man drink than go blow up the Hen-Club yuh understand? LOL.

Oh, and my good friend Wray and him Nephew came to see the New Year in with me too. Happy new year neph you soon come.

Respeck general. Stay out of Babylon's eye. Freedom Is a muss.

Uncle Leeroy

Wha gwarn family?

Imagine last week I was walking down the landing minding my business and some prick went and violated the ting again. You see how hard I was trying to keep my head down G, but you're right, sometimes you gotta let a nigga know. Yeah fam, one hench brudder try barge man on the way to the shower. So man just opened up his face ya get me?

I just come out the block now fam. I didn't wanna lose it ya nah. But I had just read one letter from my kids saying I can't speak to them till I land road. So man weren't in the mood for a next man to be acting up.

Man messed up the yute still, I don't even know who he is, all I know is that he rolls with one hype yute from North West who keeps going on funny around me. Even Marissa saw him giving me dirty looks when she came on a visit. But fuck it, it is what it is. Couple of the screws who broke it up were laughing saying welcome back Ricketts. Chatting shit about they knew I still had that fire in me. Now I'll probably get extra days on my time, so I doubt I'm seeing next summer. I'm pissed bruv, mans gotta sit in here till November.

Bro, you know you don't need to convince me of anyting. I know you're a real brudder. But you better let dem man on the outside know that you're not no rat. Cah someone somewhere's trowing dirt on your name and you gotta clean that shit up. Like yesterday. I'm not being funny but ATM wrote me the other day and he was saying some similar shit about not trusting you and how he heard you're moving funny. I know you don't like the yute but he ain't gonna come and tell me that for no reason.

Anyway my brudder, holla back.

Duane

L.O.E (Loyalty Over Everything) even money...

Yo my dargy, wha gwarn?

So what you saying now? Man are calling me a rat yeah? Lol that's some joke ting. You wanna know why man are chatting shit? Man are haters innit, that's why, they hate seeing a brother come up. It's like some crabs in a bucket mentality.

Imagine that Duane, of all people in the world man are trying to call me a funny don and a snitch. Me yuna, Redz. Lol next time tell ATM and man dem that we rep M.O.E & L.I.E – Money Over Everything & Loyalty Is Eveything!

But on the realz though, I just think man are out here hating. It's like they're confused to see a man come out of jail and do well for himself. Man in the hood are too watchy watchy. They probably just saw man driving round in my new car wearing my shirts and blazer doing my legit thing. And cos I'm not shotting no more I must be a snitch. Man are too busy preeing next man. Like they wanna know how I'm affording a Brand new X6 Bemmer with my brand new plate, when I just come out end of last year. They never thought that it could possibly be a car on finance. Fucking dickheads. Let man call me a snitch D, I ain't watching that – I'm not like these bums, I got a job.

Oh yeah, and I got a flat now, it's only temporary. It's bait still, it's across the road from Totty Police station, you know dem new flats there? Anyway I'm here for like another 3 months then I'm gonna get my permanent flat off the endz.

You was right though D, the endz is dead. I'm deffo moving out of this mix up place. There's only a few of us real ones left.

I'm glad to hear you found your balls back and finally bruck someone up. I was out ere thinking first Candy's got you Pussy whipped now prison turned you pussy LOL. Nah but real talk D I'm glad the old you isn't totally dead.

Redz

Errol,

I read your last letter over and over a while ago. Finally, I know why you left. I wanna forgive you but I'm having a hard time seeing past what I'm going through right now.

I wanna be free in every sense of the word, but when I try to fly I realise I don't know how. No one showed me how. I wish I could believe that any pain I've felt will work out for my good in the longrun. Mum said it would.

I've held this hurt in for way too long. I wish you could go back in time and take this pain away from me but I know you can't, so please help me forgive. Because I can't see how I can forgive a man who all now can't even say sorry to the boy he left behind. If you're reading this letter understand that I wanna forgive.

I don't wanna be disrespecting you no more, cos at the end of the day whether I like it or not you are my Dad. But fuck me Errol, it ain't easy to hold back on ya?

Maybe it was a bad idea to contact you while I'm in here. I just don't want it to be a thing where cos my life's a bit shitty right now that I find myself taking it all out on you. Not saying you don't deserve it but whether my frustrations are granted or not, I don't need to be carrying on like that.

Even after reading your reasons I still kinna feel like as a father you could have done more to be there to nuture what you conceived. You had time for your next family. You should of made time for us. You should of told us. Imagine if I had laid down with my sister and didn't know? Or what if I got into beef on road with my brother? You didn't think about that neither did ya.

Like I said I wanna forgive, I just need some time to decide if it's worth letting you back into my life after all these years. If I don't ever contact you again, thanks for letting me know the truth about why you left.

One last thing, make sure you write my Mum and apologise. That's the least you can do after what you've done to her. Don't think we're civil until you do that.

Gone Again.

Duane

Son,

I took your advice.

I called your Mum and apologised. Firstly, can I say how much respect I have for you as a man. It takes real courage and strength to do what you've done. I mean, I wasn't expecting an apology from you. God knows I don't deserve one but thank you all the same. If you don't mind me saying this; I'm proud to see what you've become in my absence.

The hands of time do not go back but we might just have to talk about the past to deal with the now. You're gonna have to take time to heal Duane and try learn to love yourself. I won't pretend to know you well enough to make this assumption, but maybe you can't forgive me because you haven't forgiven yourself for the mistakes you've made - maybe?

And you said no one taught you how to fly! Are you saying your Mum didn't teach you right from wrong? I'm sure Audrey would argue that she did a good job raising you as a single mother. With or without flaws that woman raised you into a man. Many single mothers have successfully raised men by themselves. They've raised young men like you who are better fathers than we were. Good men your age who have good jobs and have never been in prison.

Not saying you're not a man just because you're in prison, because we all make mistakes. I know of many great men who have been to prison and managed to turn their lives around. I have no doubts you'll do the same you just have to get yourself outta that prison you're in. But while you're waiting to be freed from the physical prison, it may do you some good to try and free yourself from the mental one - maybe?

I wanna be here to help you Duane, but I fully understand your reasons if you choose not to contact me again. I didn't realise so much scars would be open by me making contact. If I knew I would never of written you in the first place. Audrey should have never promised you that she could get my address anytime you wanted it.

Duane, if you decide not to write to me again, I would like to leave you with a piece of advice that someone once told me growing up.

God is a father to the fatherless. So if you can't have a relationship with me try talking to the big man. Ask him to give you peace and the ability to forgive. Don't feel no way to talk to him. I don't wanna sound all preachy cos I'm not the holiest person. In fact I'm one of the biggest sinners out there. But recently I've been finding that talking to God helps me through.

Do me a favour Duane, be safe and stay out of trouble. Sorry if I opened up any old wounds.

Errol

P.S. You said I can't teach you anything because you are your own man now and you're stuck in your ways. Maybe you're right Duane but that's nothing to be proud of. I was taught a man who thinks he knows it all isn't a man at all because a real man never stops learning. Don't be like me Duane, don't be the type of man who gets in his own way. I also learnt that the hard way.

Mama Can't Raise No Man

Bredrin,

Whatever you do don't write me at dat deh address in Tottenham no more.

Hear the fuckery now, Marcia only went and kick me out bredrin. Imagine. I come home early on Saturday night, I just come home from Paddy's looking forward to kicking up my 2 foot dem to watch my Match of The Day. But I never realise I never had my key on me dread.

So I go to knock on the front door and guess what? The woman put one stink sign on the door chatting bout: "Dutty bwoy Leroy, you don't live 'ere no more. Go live with the person who made you forget to come home last night."

Imagine I banged down the door bredrin and she told me say she's calling the police. Bredrin, it don't make sense in us both being in prison - someone's gotta uphold the Ricketts name. So I left her yard and walked downstairs round to the front part of her flat. Only to see the woman had dashed out my good three-piece suit and my croc shoes from her window. Belieeeve I was vex bredrin. She didn't even do me the honour of putting my tings dem in a bag – nah bredrin. She just dash it away... I all found one pigeon walking by my electric toothbrush! I was vex bredrin.

Anyway, I just called up my other woman Carolina from Sout' London and she said come. You know how I stay already Duane I always got a back up plan – mama can't raise no man but mama never raise no fool. Some call me a womaniser but that's not the trute. Uncle Lee Lee's just got a lot of love to share – That's all.

I know you don't like to take advice from your Uncle Lee. But do me one favour nephew. When you come out ah road do your best to get your own flat and don't fuck with a strong woman bredrin.

She'll take your house
She'll take your pickney dem
Your last bottle of Wray and Nephew

And your every rarse clart ting
And then dash way your heart bredrin...

I can't understand why uman leave man for cheating. Did you know that every time a male child is born in this world a next 6 girl pickney is dropping somewhere? You wanna know why the ratio is like that Duane? When God made woman for man he didn't want the man to be alone. So he made him a beautiful creature from his rib named uman. Then what did man go and do? He let woman be his temptation. So check it out now, woman ate the apple so her curse was to be temptation for all man kind and for her to have to deal wid next woman tryna teef her man. You don't see the fuckery us men have to put up with.

If Monica my first wife did understand this logic then I wouldn't be sofa surfing at 58 years of age. Imagine if Eve never did eat the apple, now me and Monica would still be together. I'm vex Mon left me and took the kids dem. But me still love errr dread me love errr.

Guidance me nephew – walk strong.

Uncle Leeroy

P.S. Don't tell nobody I said I still love my first wife. It's been a long day for me dread I don't feel like myself, it muss be the Wray talking.

Mama Can't Raise No Man

Yo Errol,

I'm glad to hear you said sorry to my Mum. Real talk, cos if you said you couldn't do that then me and you couldn't ever chat again.

And why you trying to do an Audrey on me? Coming at me with all that Bible bashing business? You're a bit bright to be telling me that God's a father to the fatherless. These times I can't even see you. You're like some ghostwriter bruv. You see when you don't grow up with a Dad yeah, it's not easy to let anyone else take that place.

As a fatherless child there's been times I've found it hard just to believe that God even exist. So telling me God's a father to the fatherless ain't gonna help me out mate.

A brother's got some form of trust issues. It's a struggle to trust or follow what I can't see. They say a son's first God or hero is meant to be his dad. I always found it funny that Mum wanted me to believe that my father in heaven loved me, while accepting that you, my father in Harlesden didn't give a F.... real talk Errol. I've always known deep down I needed you to be around in my life. You asked if my Mum didn't show me right from wrong. And the answer to that would be yes she tried. But define right and wrong?

Mum did what she could to set me on the right path but it didn't work out. Even though she showed me right from wrong I always fucked up at the crossway when I had to decide between right and left. That's where you were meant to come in Errol. I've always thought a man's role was to guide his children but specialise in guiding his son. Y'know, cos a father's got that male instinct. I really missed this guidance growing up.

As a Dad I've had my bad days - the days when you feel the stress mounting. Certain mornings I look out of my cell window and I think: "Dad you're a dickhead!" Cos I see what you did, you took the easy option, you just ran away. There's nuff man who have struggled with becoming fathers and the responsabilities that follow but us real men don't buss out. And I know I'm my own man, I'm responsible for my own actions. but I still can't help thinking if you was there to teach me and love me, I wouldn't of made as much mistakes as I did.

What I'm saying is I'm ready to try ah ting and face my demons like a man. I don't wanna come out on road, see you by chance and feel to box you down. Nah, I wanna be calm if I ever happen to see you in person. So let's do this now while I'm in the mood to open up. By the way I still don't want no relationship with you. I just want that father to son convo but without the titles. You know, that man-to-man back to basics stuff. Anyway the ball's in your court now......

Hit me back up whenever you're ready. No rush as you can see man aint going nowhere for now – bless up Errol.

Duane

Mama Can't Raise No Man

Bruv,

Why you writing to me on some 'I told you so' tip. I come to you for help and all you wanna do is tell me how your spirit never took to Jermome. Do you really think that shit's helping right now. Do you even know what kinda stress I'm dealing with right now.

I called Jerome the other day and the boy couldn't even talk properly he sounded high off ah something. At the moment I can't tek the headache. I mean honestly I'm a mess right now bruv. I'm trying to juggle work, maintain my daughter, maintain a house and do well at Uni. Let alone deal with my own issues and emotions. And then I have to deal with my emotional rollercoaster of a babyfather? And on top of that you wanna talk about you're not surprised because his parents were fiends. Really?!

Everyone I see is telling me Jermone's acting like a mad man - just bare aggressive. Talk on road is he owes every weed man in Totty money.

I need you to stop coming at me with all of your high-horse Dr Freud theories and write to him for me D. I mean as soon as. Destiny needs her Dad. And I don't know why but I'm worried something bad is gonna happen to him, then Destiny won't have a dad. So please just do me a favour and write him without any threats or hype talk. Just try get him to see sense. He won't tell you but I know he looks up to you just like ATM does.

I tried my best to show Jerome love you know Duane. But ever since his Mum walked out, his Dad never showed him no love, he don't know how to act. He makes out that he cheated on me cos I didn't show him no love after Destiny was born. He's chatting shit. It wasn't the lack of love I was showing him; it was the fact that my love was never enough. He was crying out for the love of his mum cos she left him. I could never give him that. How could I have ever replaced a mother's love? I know he's had it hard but he never tries to fight his demons like a man should and become the partner and Dad that I know deep down he wants to be.

Even though we were friends for 3 years before Destiny was born I still don't feel like I really knew Jerome. No matter how much I tried to be there for him when we was together he wouldn't let me. Whenever he was down he didn't bring it to me, he would just bill a spliff or leave the yard, he weren't like this before Destiny.

I don't even know why I bothered writing to you after your last letter. I just hope you're done with your psychological analysis of Jermone coz right about now, we need your help.

Marissa

P.S. On a lighter tip, hear what your niece said to me today: "Can you tell Uncle Duane to hurry up and come home so we can play Connect 4, and that I love him."

Yo Sis,

I know you're vex with your baby farder but don't take it out on me. I'm just trying to help you the best way I know and you got jokes about you don't need my psychological analysis. It ain't about that Sis, I'm just trying to help you understand where the yute's coming from. Remember he's 22 not that I'm defending his fuckery antics.

But in Jerome's defence the scars that he's got are deeper than most. He needs time to get his head right. You can't replace a mother when his Mum loved crack more than she loved him. And now that you've left him it's probably bunning Jerome so much that it's sent him on a mad one. I'm not saying you're wrong to leave and I'm not saying feel sorry for him. Just try understanding the levels he's facing and not take it personally. You don't have to empathise with him just understand enough about him for Destiny's sake.

I know I don't tell you this but I'm nuff proud of you sis, you're a real strong sister, mother and women and you have to fight to stay that way. Jerome might never be grown enough for you or Destiny, but as long as you always keep the door open for him to see his yute then you're doing your part.

Dr. Freud

P.S. Tell my Niece I said I wanna play Connect 4 too. And when I finally come out of this shithole we can play Connect 4 all day if she likes. Obviously don't tell her I said shithole or all day because she'll hold me to that lol. Love sis – stay up.

Duane,

I hope you're good D. It's been time bro, nearly a whole year. I took your advice from your last letter and put my head in my books. So I'm just waiting to get my results now, I need at least a 2.1 but I hope I passed with a first.

I'm back in Totty now, how are you though? I heard from the girls that Candy's still nowhere to be seen. That shit must be really bunning you. I can't imagine having children and my baby-father taking them from me for a year. This is all too crazy to make sense of. All I know is that you must of really broke my friend's heart bad.

Oh yeah, the girls were telling me that Candy blocked my number and that she ain't chatting to me cos she thinks I'm taking your side, I dunno where she got that foolishness from probably that bitterhearted sister of hers. Lorna's probably the reason you were not seeing the kids in the first place, once she gets into Candy's head it's nothing but problems. But it's cool cos I'm back in London now so I'm bound to bump into Candy one of these days. And when I do we can deal with this in person. I don't business whether she's talking to me or not you both made me God-Mother and I wanna see how my God-Children are doing.

On another note D, why the fuck are all you men dogs? Believe I just found out my man was cheating on me with some any random girl on campus.

I'm not even hurt no more, he can bounce. But I don't know why you brothers can't just be loyal ffs. I mean I'm 25 now I ain't got no kids yet and my clock is ticking.

I know you're my boy and everything D but even you need to grow up now and stop flinging it about. Don't think Candy hasn't told me about all of your darg moments. She told me all the shit you was doing with next gyal. Believe it or not if it wasn't for me telling her not to leave you and to give you time to grow she would of left your ass years ago.

Real talk bro you had my friend's heart in your hand, she was all about Duane. You messed up bad, but you did manage to give up selling drugs so I believe one day you will manage to give up being a hoe too. LOL.

Sorry to be so blunt but I can't sit here feeling sorry for you when I know you aint no angel. Don't take it personal bro it's not just you one, look at my guy Kevin, most of you brothers are dogs. You lot need to man up and 'llow the little games you play with girls' hearts.

Don't get sour at anything I said in this letter. Make sure you write me back and I'll keep a look out for Candy. Still love you my Darg

T X

Wha gwan Teah,

It's been a minute for true. Glad to hear you finished Uni now. All
that hard works gonna pay off just wait and see.

And how you mean don't get sour by your words. I aint got the
energy to be sour, your opinion's your opinion innit. I know you're
a real person who always speaks their mind and I respect that still.
But why you gotta be like that? You need to drop me out with that
all men are dogs chat.

I don't care what Candy told you about me. Look how long you've
known me, I'm not half as bad as I used to be. And I'm fed up of the
way women never take no responsibility for your part in a break up.
You lot never look at what you do to hurt men. Nah it's always the
man's fault. I don't know nothing about your boy or why he cheated.
All I know is I'm grown enough to say man fucked up innit, but that
don't make me a dog. I just feel like we mis-learned manhood.

I know whatever I write in defence is gonna be seen as excuses.
I expect that, but to me a reason only becomes an excuse when
you've stopped trying to figure out what lays beanaeth the reason.

There are two kinds of men that I know who cheat. The man who
cheats when he feels disrespected or unappreciated on a regular.
Or the man who's just an outright dog and he can't help himself.

The question you sista's need to ask is: what type of man did/do
you have? I can't defend all men everywhere, but I've learned from
my own mistakes that you can't show love if you don't know love.

I know you probably don't wanna hear what I'm saying so I'll just
leave it there.

Write me back when you're ready.

Duane

Hi Nephew,

How you doing? I heard from your sister that Candy has stopped communication with your children again, I'm sorry to hear that. I notice when I write to you, you never get back until I write you a second time? I'm starting to think maybe it's my approach. Maybe you're getting fed up with me writing you telling you what you need to do and how to carry yourself. I'm guessing you don't wanna hear it from me?

Well if so, tough. I can't help but be forward and direct with you Neph cos that's my way of love.

I can't lie Duane, recently I've been worried about you and so is your Mum and so is your sister. I want to be there for you Duane. But no one can be there for you if you keep shutting the people you care about out. If you carry on doing that, you're gonna end up lonely and miserable just like Uncle Leroy. I do not want to see you self-destruct like that.

What's really bothering you Duane?

Are you O.K? I mean emotionally, spiritually?

I know you've always found it hard to express yourself, but I need you to try. Do you remember as a little boy you use to get angry and then cry when nobody was listening? Well I do, and I remember giving you pen and some paper and telling you to write down how you're feeling. You always gave me back the paper with a poem of your thoughts.

Every time without fail I was blown away by your ability to express yourself through words. I know you hate writing, let alone poems, but if I could just ask you to write me a poem of what's bothering you then maybe I can help somehow.

One more thing I want to know if you've been reading the books I've been sending you. Have you received them?

Tell me sutten, cos I'm curious to know. I wanna know what you think of yourself when you look in the mirror? Cos whenever I look at you I see a King who hasn't realised his full potential. What do you see?

Walk safe Nephew X

Hi Duane,

How you doing, it's me Errol. Just a quick one...

What did you learn about manhood that your Mum couldn't teach you? I'm not sure if I'm hearing you right but do you really believe that your Mum didn't play a role in making you the man you are today?

If so, please, I want you to speak your mind and say what you feel about how you were raised. And I fully understand if you don't wanna feel like your bad talking your Mum, but just tell me how she raised you. Bear in mind I would never pass judgement on your Mother because I left her in the situation. What type of things did she use to do growing up?

What exactly was missing? What was it that Audrey couldn't do that you think as a father I could?

And another thing I would like to know, why don't you talk to your Mum? How do you cut people off so easy?

And if you're saying your Mum couldn't raise you – then who did?

Sorry if it seems like I'm going on with the questions, I just gotta know what's going on in your head. And what a man is to you?

Anyway Duane like I said it's just a quick one. Hope to hear from you soon – I would say if you need anything just ask but I know you won't so – stay safe...

Errol

Errol,

You know what, I had to take a minute to think about what I really missed. Cos, how can I know what's missing if I never had it to miss?

All I'm saying is Mum couldn't teach me to be one, end of. Most single mothers I knew growing up had this concept of what it is to be what they call a 'real man'. The joke is everything they've learnt about what being a 'real man' is they've learned from another woman or society. And I for one don't agree with a lot of their ideas of what being a man is.

How did Mum raise me? Mum raised me the best she knew how, but I would say she lost control of me before I hit the teenage stage. My Mum was two different people: one minute she was caring and the next she was the crazy shouting woman, wildin' out. It just didn't make sense to me as a boy child. Growing up Mum had, what I felt at the time, were all these strict rules.

From young Mum was on to me, she made sure I did my homework and my house chores every day before I even thought about asking her to go out and play. And if I didn't have homework she would make homework for me, LOL. I know why she was doing that now but at age 10 I just wanted to get out there and be free.

Mum was trying to mould me into a good man from early. Constant drilling in my head about how I had to be responsible, have manners, be counted for and I learned a lot from that. We had a good relationship as mother and son and at times your absence didn't even cross my mind because Mum's love was enough. Anything within reason that I wanted for Christmas or my bday, if Mum could afford it she'd get it for us even if it meant getting it late.

I can't say I ever went a birthday without a cake or a Christmas without something under the Christmas tree.

Mum lived by the saying 'Spare the rod, spoil the child.' And I have to commend her for doing her best to raise me into a respectable boy.

But I didn't always respect her authority - I struggled to see her sense. Past a certain age Mum couldn't get through to me. She couldn't understand why I was getting so lippy. She use to say:

"Don't think cos you're taller than me I won't jump up and lick you down." LOL. But even she knew the licks weren't affecting me anymore.

Like some days I would come home late from school and Mum would cuss me out for not coming straight home to change my clothes and do my homework and chores. But by the time I reached year 9 she kind of got fed up of being so strict. And where I always use to question her rules and say she's being unfair she kind of just gave in and stopped nagging me about certain things. It's like she knew I was lying when I made the same excuses for coming in late after school but because she couldn't prove it she just let it slide more often. She couldn't be bothered to fight with me every day over the same thing. I wore her down. She would be coming in from work some days so tired that she just couldn't be bothered to cuss me.

I don't know how to answer this question, Errol. The best way I can sum it up today is confirmation is what was missing from you. Confirmation of what a man is.

Imagine if you stayed to raise me? Rather than allowing the streets' perception of manhood to confuse my head. When I was younger, the word roadman didn't exist. But as I grew in to my late teens, without actually realising it, that's the type of man – a road man – is what I was becoming.

And now look at me; a man who's back in jail over some bullshit, trying to figure out if I'll ever be able to represent to my children what I now know manhood to truly be.

It's long writing Errol, this is hurting my head and I don't know if I'm even making any sense – chat more soon.

Duane

Hi Aunty Jan, I hope you're well

When I look in the mirror what do I see?

I see a man the image of me.

A man with black skin, and a frown of confusion, wondering if this mirror's an illusion.

When I look in the mirror what do I see?

Sometimes I look but I don't just see me!

I stare in my eyes and see through to my soul, but is my soul pure? Boy who really knows?

I see potential and a weight on my shoulder, some say it's a chip, but it's more like a boulder.

When I'm out on the wing just minding my biz, I've seen an older first meeting his kid.

I'm not even fazed by most things that I see, what's Man meant to say, ahhh shit - that's so sweet? Father and son reunited at last, we are numb to most feelings, man don't give a rarse.

All over this jail there's plenty more brothers who don't know their Dad they just know their Mother.

When I'm back in my cell I still see my olders, the mirrors reflection from over my shoulder.

When I look in the mirror I day dream envisions, I see the mandem sitting in prison.

It feels like we're stuck in this 2nd place living, we all make mistakes but no one's ever forgiven.

There's misguided pride and a heart full of bravery, when I look in the mirror I see mental slavery.

Invisible shackles keep holding me down – making it harder to picture my crown.

When I look in the mirror there's things that I like but that vision gets tarnished by stereotypes......

Let me say what you see when you're looking at me
You see a thug, with a long CRB.

You see my past my prior convictions
So you stain my name and keep me restricted.

You know what Aunty, I don't even wanna carry on with this poetry stuff. Let's just say I'm fed up of being seen as a threat or less of a person when all I want is a fair chance at life.

I'm more than just a roadman. I'm more than a Nigga. I do see my potential; it's just getting harder to see the light at the end of the tunnel.

Yeah and I have been getting the books you've sent me on black history and empowerment. I'm not really one for reading more time.

Plus I'm not ready for all that right now. I got other stuff on my mind. It don't make sense in me making a promise to do some book club with you and then not stick to it. Sorry Aunty Jan I'm just keeping it real. But if you want you can keep sending them to me. You never know, when the time's right, I might just pick up one and read it. I got 9 months left, anything can happen.

Oh yeah you asked how I'm doing emotionally and spiritually, that question threw me off a bit. To answer it though I would say I'm emotionally deflated and spiritually confused. But I'll find my way don't worry about nothing.

Duane

Hi Nephew,

Duane, I read your letter this morning; I respect your honesty. It's better to hear you be a man of your word rather than committing to something you know you won't do. So I salute you for your continuous growth young King. You go and take time to mend your broken wings. I will continue to send a book every month and randomly check on you between to see how you're doing whether you write me back or not.

And that poem there, boy that was something else Duane. Now I understand what you see. All I can say is that maybe the mirror is showing an illusion. Maybe it would be helpful if you change the way you look at things. If you feel the world see's you as just another 'nigga' or 'roadman' then that's the mental slavery shackles you need to be released from. Only you can free you by changing the way you view yourself and your brothers. Regardless of how the world see's you, if people can't see the greatness within you that's their loss not yours.

Keep your head up Duane, you're a greater man than you think you are. Love you D.

Aunty Jan X

My little brother it's PJ.

I know I ain't been in contact with you for the last 8 years bruh, but I had to ghost. Don't take it personal, no-one ain't heard from me since my Mum died. I had to get my mental right to focus on this bird. By the way thanks for the letter you sent when Mum died. You really got a way with words and it helped me to think.

I was in my cell the other day doing the maths to remember how old you are now. I know when I first come prison you was what? 14? I've rid like 11 and a half years now. So what, that must make you 25? Madness how the time's gone. Over the years I've been on the wing and heard certain man from my era chatting your name, I had to laugh still. Cos I remember the same little Duane running around in his Arsenal kit on the Farm. The same boy I used to send to the shop and let keep the change and buy a sweet for himself. What always made me laugh about you was whenever you came back from the shop you never got yourself nothing. Most other 11 year olds would of spent the change one time. But nah, not you. You use to take the change and save that. From those days I knew you was different from the other yutes on the estate. I all remember one time I sent you shop for me and with the change you bought some pasta and tuna fish. Me and my bredrins were benning up, until you said it was for your Mum to cook that night. I'm telling you lickle bro as funny as it looked, after you said that all us olders on the block rated you. That's why I named you Lickle-Big-Man. I made sure everyone knew who you was so know one on the farm would trouble you.

I remember when you turned 13 you asked me if you could move work for me, and I said no! I see you were going places, and I wanted you to see it too. But being the little man you are you went behind my back and still found a next older to put you on the game. What was his name again? I can't even remember, but the way I clapped up that Yardy man for giving you that food was class-A. Not glorifying my actions just letting you know why I did it.

Who would of ever thought the man would have run and told police that I clapped him and get me a year in H.M.P! I weren't too bothered when I got that bird there, at the time I was just happy to know I helped stop you from getting into the road-life us man were living. I knew that life wasn't for you. Even though you were eager for the paper. What you couldn't see with your young eyes was that everything that glitters isn't gold.

So imagine how vex I was when I came back on road to hear you had a line and was moving white at 14. I felt like I did a year in jail for nothing. Not blaming you either little bro, cos I never told you why I went jail in the first place. That's why when I saw you I told you, you can't move white. I understood I wasn't your Dad to be telling you that plus I understood you was like a younger me, too stubborn to listen. So I gave you the link to the High-Grade man. And helped you build the line with the right clientele. Then I taught you how to move properly cos before I heard you were moving like Mr Bean on road, baiter than bait.

I'm not writing to reminisce or nothing. I'm writing for other reasons. Little bro, you know the streets talk and so do the prisons. So even though I've been in here 11 years now I still know a bit about a bit. I think it was the 1st year into my sentence I heard you ended up in Feltham for your first sentence at age 15 for moving bait. Then 10 years into my sentence one younger your age who got 25 to life told me that you came off the roads. And how Classford got you a job working with Broadwater Farm youth football team and you had a next job driving or something. I can't lie to you Lickle Big Man, that news made me feel a different type of joy, I knew you finally got the message.

So when I heard of the news that my little brother Duane is back in jail for the 3rd time I was baffed. Why would this boy change his life around only to do a bird for some younger. But Duane, I get it. You feel part responsible for bringing him on the road, just as I did for giving in and bringing you on the road. This younger must be more than just some younger for you to take the fall. A part of me admires you for that cos I would've never done that for my youngers - unless it was you.

Now I'm older I look at things differently. My loyalty doesn't lie in the streets or behind these prison walls that confine me. But instead it lays in me. I would never advise you to go back and snitch on your younger. What is done is done but what I will say is that if you're trying to be a different type of man you might find it easier to drop certain people out. Even the one's you got love for. When you get back on road you gotta put your family first. Don't feel like you're in any kind of loyal debt to your younger either. He's old enough to make his own choices.

On the subject of this Younger you're looking out for. I've heard this kid's name ringing bells amongst big man older than me. And these fellow lifers really wanna hurt him. I just wanted to write you and tell you if you can save him from himself then do so, but if you can't when you come out, live your life. Cos like I've been saying to you from day one, you're much better than this lifestyle so don't end up like me.

I got another 14 years to go until being considered for parole. Inshallah if I ever come out of here I want to see you've done something with your life – the world is yours young brother. I practice Islam now and I don't get into drama unless someone comes at me. I try to walk in peace but because of my past in here everyone either loves me or hates me. I hear from the streets there's little youngers on the block as young as 16 saying "free PJ he's the King of Totty." These people are lost. How can I be the King of a place which is gonna take 25 years of my life? I may never see Tottenham again and if I do, it sure won't be the same.

Do me a favour Little Big Man, I don't want my legacy to be King of Totty. So when you get home let whoever needs to know I'm not the King of nothing, I'm not a legend for what I did. Furthermore, let them know that I'm in here preaching Allah to other young murderers to let them know there is hope. Let them know I don't even go by the name PJ no more, I am no longer him.

Glad to know you see the big picture. I'm gonna go and read my Qu'ran where I find peace. Keep walking in peace Lickle Big Man, and I'll see you when I get out. Inshallah.
Pierre

Man like PJ una!

I really wasn't expecting a letter from you.

Time's definitely passed quick. I know you ain't gonna respond to this letter but I'm gonna write it anyway.

You know what P I never knew why you went prison back in the day. I never knew the first time you went jail you went for beating up Yardy Reggie. And I damn sure never knew you beat him up cos he put me on to this trap life. Now it makes sense why dem man run Reggie out the block and told me to stay away from him. As a yute I heard he was a snitch but I never knew why. I never knew you went to those extremes to keep me off road. Imagine if I saw what you were trying to show man back then? I got mad respect for you Big P seriously.

Your letter took me down memory lane. I was 10 years old when you first spoke to me. I had just scored a sick goal and you was like: Oi! my yute that was heavy. Yo darg, my ego went from 0-100 and I scored a few more. I saw how people engaged with you on the estate. It was mad, you was like some kinda general, but not in a bully type way. Everyone knew that you couldn't say Broadwater Farm without saying PJ first. But man outside Tottenham either had you down as a King or a villain. To me though at 10 you were just that bless older on the estate who sent me or my friends shop and let us keep the change. It's only when I hit secondary school when I clocked how you acquired that change.

Then a couple years later I wanted to be like you. I wanted to eat like a king. I wanted to walk road like you, talk like you. Get love in the hood like you did. Drive the same type of cars, wear the same gold chains, and bring the rest of the village with me. I couldn't be Lickle Big Man anymore, I wanted to be Big Man D.

So when I asked to be your worker and you said no I thought you were trying to get in the way of my ambitions, which is why I went round you and made some bad mistakes. Can you believe I had to get set up, shot, stabbed, bury couple of my bredrins, have police run up in my yard, and face prison twice before the penny started to drop! All of that just to be the big man. What a waste of life.

You're right though, I still have time on my side and as long as I have time the world is mine. When I really sit and think about the time left you have to ride, it reminds me that I need to get back and focus so I don't get a 25 myself.

Oh yeah, I love the fact you're preaching to other prisoners to leggo the road-man-tality. I can't picture it myself but that's a good look big bro.

And I hear what you're saying about rectifying your legacy as Big PJ. Don't watch nothing, I got you. You deserve to be remembered for the man you are today. A man who made some bad choices in the past for which he is paying the price. A man who has not only taken responsibility for his actions, but a man who has learned from them also. A man who has remorse and doesn't find glory in his past actions. A man who finds peace in making peace.

I tell you what big bro I respect you now more than I ever have. If I can become just half the man you've become when I lann road, I'll be set for life. No doubt.

Duane

P.S.
You said something that's always stuck with me.

"D, I prefer to be a man with a heart of flesh than a man with a heart of stone.

The man with the heart of stone is a liability. He may appear hard on the outside, but on the inside he doesn't know himself. A person is pronounced dead once their heart stops working.

Then you got the man with a heart of flesh. He may appear weak on the outside and he may also be a liability, the man with a heart of flesh will endure much more pain. But, at least the man with a heart that works will be able to feel joy when it comes."

I didn't get it back then, but I get it now G.

Thanks for showing love over the years. And thanks for always keeping it 100 with man. You'll always be a legend in my eyes. See you on the other side PJ. Sorry I mean Pierre Johnson.

Big Brudder 4 life...

Sis,

If I'm honest you might need to just drop out the idea of Jerome coming to see Destiny and do you. I don't know what you've done to this brudder but this guy's lovestruck. Always leave the door open but explain to Destiny that my man's not too well right now. Love's a funny thing you know sis.

Imagine I woke up last night and see my cell mate hanging himself with his bed sheets. I tried to lift him but I woke up too late. I was just baffed sis, cos this brudders forever cracking joke in here. Of all the people I've shared a cell with he's the last man I would've had on the suicide watch.

He left a note titled. Give this to my people. I saw it and it was sad to read still. It said:

I can't go on like this. First she broke up with me and that was hard but I got past that. Then she breeded for a next man and that was hard but I got past that. Now the bitch says she thinks its best I don't see or speak to my own kids no more and how she's moving to Brazil with my kids, what the hell can I do with that?

I can't wait 11 more years to get out of here and go fucking South America to find two 14 year olds, they'll never remember me. That's even if I can find them.

Sorry Mum I can't do this no more, I tried.

Yeah madness this week in H.M.P. Anyway I hope all is well big ed will speak soon.

In a bit

Duane

Yo lickle brudder?

I know you ain't heard from me in a minute, but I was still vex with you. Even after reading your letter, you just trigger off the trigger in me. I forgive you for barking at man though. But do me a favour, don't ever forget yourself again. I let you bite man once because of everything that was going on but next time round I won't hesitate to bite back. But it's all love my brudder.

The other day I got a letter from one oldler I use to look up to. You know the one everyone calls the legend on the Northside of T, the legend PJ. Or I should say Pierre.

Yeah, I weren't expecting that one as we aint spoke for years. But PJ, I mean Pierre's really changed his outlook on life as a man.

He's moving like me, you could say, other than his beliefs. Man like PJ aint on it no more. Same things I'm preaching to you he's co-signing with me. So I think it's about time you respect me for the man I'm trying to be in 'ere and respect the ting when I say leave my beef or any other beef alone.

I'm telling you my G the trapping life has no promise, it's an in and out game – get in and get out. You're still young you got time to go college and re-align yourself in the system. You don't wanna be 25 and have an empty CV.

Oh yeah before I forget, you see Redz? Whatever you hear about him it aint true so dead all that talk now. I don't like using this word anymore but you need to understand the levels, you see that Nigga Redz, he's 100. When I'm in here on my face he's the one sending money through my sister's door. That dudes 100.
Duane

P.S. I hope you and the mother of your Angel are OK. Like I said last time, everything happens for a reason. Keep your head up little bro. Be safe. #LeggoDaRoads

Duane

I got some real bad news for you bro. Your boys Anton (ATM) and Gavin (GTM) got shot earlier today. ATM's in hospital but Gavin didn't make it, he died on the spot. I'm sorry bruv. What do you want me to do? Let me know if you need me to do anything.

Rissa X

Marissa,

What the fuck's going on out there?

So man just killed off my lickle bredrin like that! Like it's nothing.

I heard a man in here last night saying some yutes got licked down in T town but I never thought it was one of my lickle dargs dem. I can't believe this shit. Do me a favour and take this letter to the hospital for ATM please.

Duane

Yo my brudder,

Glad to know you're still breathing. Imagine I sent you a letter the same day you got hit. I didn't know wha gwarn then but I know wha gwarn now. Marrissa told me everything...

All I can say darg is I'm sorry for your loss. I really did like GTM he was a good yute still. I know it's gonna be hard right now, but try and be grateful you're still alive G. And if I was you, when I come out of hospital I would get the hell out of the ends. Go clear your head before you do a mad one. I've been there already darg, truss me. Understand you're not gonna be in a good place mentally for a minute. And while you're mourning and healing up you need to take time out.

Write me back and give it to Rissa she'll post it for me.

Duane

Duane,

Wha gwarn five-star general?

Hear wha gwan now me nephew. The other night I did go out to shake two leg with the boys dem. We went to some big peoples dance. It was my bredrins wife's 50th. So anyway now the last thing I remember I was whining up with some pretty gyal in the red dress. Then the next thing I remember bredrin I was rubbing out mi y'eye dem waking up in some random bedroom. Bredrin, when I woke up all I could see was pink wall paper and pink curtains tu-rarse. I didn't know what the rarse was going on dred. I could just feel this whale of a woman laying on my arm, she nearly did dead off my arm bredrin. No circulation none.

Vex I'm vex you wouldn't be-lieve. When I see the face on her I was vex bredrin. She looked like me with weave bredrin. I'm telling you she weren't the same empress I was whining up with. The cheek of it is the woman was laying there next to me smiling in a deep sleep like sutten did sweet her. Like say she just won the jackpot bredrin. If you ever did see the way I slid out and rolled off that bed bredrin. It took a lot of tekkers to creep out the yard bredrin. Sometime my boys Wray and him Nephew let me drink too much.

Anyway lemme talk up the tings about why women don't rate us. In slavery days the women saw the slave master as the head not their own man. The slave owner dem would rape our women and beat us like animals in front of them. And nothing has changed years after its just psychological now. In this ere 21st century when a black man wants to lead his family, a sister will look to society and follow that lead instead of her own man. And if there's a break up and fight over seeing the pickney dem, that women will run to her head master again - the police, the courts, the system which again gives her the power over him to lead that family. If a man can't do his natural thing and lead his family, then what is he to do?

You can't replace a mother our mothers are key. But so are we fathers.
Uncle Leeroy

Duane,

I went to visit ATM yesterday and gave him the letter.

He's in North Mid Hospital and he doesn't look too good. The scar he's gonna get after the stitches is gonna be serious. You should see how open he is. And when I went there police were sitting outside the hospital ward outside the corridor. They must be armed police cos a few of them had guns. I don't know what's going on but Anton says he will write you. I'll come back in the week to post it if I have to.

It must be hard to be a brother in this day and age. Just seeing ATM lying there reminded me of what it was like when you got shot, it was horrible. I don't know how you guys do this roadman stuff. Tell me something, what's it like for you? I mean what's it like in jail Duane. You've been there 3 times and you've never spoken to me about it but I wanna know, what do you do from day to day? How do you get by? Tell me what it's like bruv.

P.S.

I'm not gonna chase down Jerome to come look for his daughter, but I will never stop him. And I texted him and let him know my door is always open for him to come get her. Sorry to hear about your cell mate killing himself. Just goes to show how much you guys deal with.

Don't ever let life get you that low bruh, I'm always here. Love You.

Marissa X

Nephew,

Hear wha gwarn now...

Whatever you do don't write me at that there address in South.
Guess what happen now. So remember that same night I did tell
you how I end up at the woman's house by accident? Alright well
next morning I come home to Mandy's flat and tried to sleep off
the drink and that. Then next thing bredrin I felt some cold water
over my face. I jumped up like ah wha de rarse. Then I see this mad
woman standing with an empty Dutch-Pot dripping the remains
of the water. Vex I was vex bredrin I wanted to box her down
immediately dred. But you know I don't do dem tings dere.

So hear the motive behind the fuckry now. She try ask me where
was I last night. Kmt. I told her I went to Reggie's yard after
the party. Then she said stop tell lie, then she dashed my new
blackberry at me. Bredrin I couldn't argue properly true I was still
hung-over. But hear Mandy to me 'what's this then?'

Duane, I look pon my screen and see a picture with me and Miss
thunder pants with the pink curtains and shit. So these times now
I'm vex bredrin, then at the bottom of the screen she texted thanks
for last night Mr Loverman.

I got nyam red handed dread but from what I remember I never
even slept with Miss Mampy. Well I can't remember but I don't have
any damage to say it happened. I turned to Mandy and said it wasn't
me. Then she told me to come out of her yard. So I said fuck it and
went to my next woman's yard uppa Harlesden. Yeah I'm living up
North West by Carolina's now.

Told you neph this is why you can't have just one woman. They're
too temperamental. You can't put all your chicks in one stable. One
minute dem love you, then the next minute it's come out my yard.
But it's cool cos I did like the bookies down here better anyway.

Write me back general. (My new address is Church Road NW10)
Uncle Leeroy

Mama Can't Raise No Man

Yo Duane,

Bruv they killed my boy. Just shot him in broad daylight on the
block, in front of the little yutes dem. It was mental bruv.
GTM must of saw dem buss the corner under the garages on the
block. He must of clocked them rolling up in their rusty. At the time
I was slipping, I was looking in the opposite direction. I heard him
shout: "Anton, Anton,"

But I aired him cos I'm a stubborn fuck. We said we would never
call each other by our governments when we're on the roads,
unless it's a life or death situation. But I forgot the unless part.

I heard two shots lick off then I remembered the unless part to the
code. I turned around as quick as I could fam. I see GTM running
towards me just over an arms length away from me. Then I heard
couple more shots pop off – one hit my rib. Then I felt GTM tackle
me to the floor. I heard 7 more shots then the next thing I know
I'm waking up in this hospital hearing my boy's dead.

I can't believe GTM's dead blud, he took seven shots in the back,
The blood was all over me. I've got clean clothes on today, but I'm
still feeling dirty, cos now I got my bredrins bloods stains all over
my conscious.

His Mum blames me. She said it should've been me.

Everything's fucked up D, the dreams over now. Fuck it I'm not even
going to the funeral. And you know what she's right to blame me.
If I wasn't going on so rowdy moving to certain man for you then
they wouldn't have come back on man like that. It's my fault. Them
bullets had my name on it G. But GTM jumped in front to move me
and he took the other six that were for me. I can't believe it. He
was just there. I can't believe it.

I gotta discharge myself. They got feds outside my ward and shit.
You're right I need to go cunch and get my P up. I might go when
I leave here. You said that before. See if I listened, me and GTM
could've been off the radar living life.

Fuck M.O.E what's Money without my brother GTM?

You're in jail because of my food. My best friend is dead cos of my beef. I fucked the dream up. I am so sorry bro.

ATM

Bruv,

Right now you're flames on the roads. You've been bait for a minute. Try know for the next few months you're gonna be under obo. Boi-dem are watching you bredrin.

You might be one step ahead of them for now, but you can't always stay a step ahead. Remember it's your one brain on road working against six or seven man in a room planning to get you. It's like cat and mouse when you're out there trappin' you're the mouse. We all know two heads are better than one. So the feds might let you leave the hospital without questioning because they know you're gonna go back to trappin' and that's when you get trapped. I've been in this game for years fam, I learned shit the hard-way. A fiend will inform on you bro, there's no love in this. If you've got something to lose in life leave the drug game alone.

Try know this, Boi dem don't like what you're doing, your girl don't like what you're doing, your mum don't like what you're doing. And when you were doing tings you were being loud about it, like you were proud. Dead that behaviour. Don't be a man who no one can reason with. Don't be a rebel without a cause.

And you see what GTM's marjey said to you don't take it on. I understand how she feels but that's not your burden to carry. Everyman on road knows the repercussions of being on the road. They're harsh and they can be deadly. So don't blame yourself no more, cos GTM wouldn't blame you. Don't let his Mum's words get to you. Go up cunch for a year; bring the missus if you can. Take time out bro but don't hide from the funeral. He was your bonafied everyone knew that. If you don't go you might always regret that too.

I have regrets. Like all the time I've wasted in jail. Every day is a reminder of time passing that me and my yutes could have played, and that's why I'm trying to move different now. I need to get out early on tag and make up for the lost time. Even if that means getting a little job in a factory stacking shelves. Seriously I over think in here. Like if I was to add the number of years all of the mandem my age from the block spent in jail we would have done a couple hundred years in total. Don't do anything wreckless to add to that number. Don't worry if man think you're moist cos the only opinion that matters is yours.

You don't have to shot no more G. I know it's hard out 'ere but do you ever think about working? Or do you wanna be trapping forever? I'm not judging your choices but if you could, would you work? Don't get caught up in this system and become another statistic.

Heal up quick my brudder and go up North to lay low.

Duane

Yo Duane,

Thanks for the heads up on the obo. You're right Duane, it's about getting in, then getting out. The game is dead without GTM next to me but I just got a few more rolls to make until I'm 100.

When I finish playing this game of snakes and ladders, don't think I'm coming off roads to look a job. Nah darg man ain't feeling that. I know man my age working their ass off for minimum wage. The way my line is set up right now, it wouldn't even make sense to knock the hustle just yet. Try know I'm making more P's in a week than man my age are making in a month? I can't drop the hustle like that darg. But I'll be more hush about it.

I dunno about you bruv, but I don't believe in going backwards. Man can't go from pushing whips to a push bike. I'm not on it my darg. I'm 18 now, man can't go back to jumping on the buses G. And look how much enemies I got! Nah dead that, in war you can't be broke, man need that Victoria out here. But I do hear what you're saying darg, I'll buss out to cunch next month no doubt.

You know me already D, I can't work for no one. I ain't putting on no suit or tie to go make money for someone else. I'm comfortable just doing me. Man's different like that. I'm a dream chaser. Man want dem Alan Sugar businesses, that Warren Buffet paper and an Island like Richard Branson's. You know dem way dere?

Don't watch nothing though cuz, I soon hit the belly and leave all this shit behind. I got this. You good for money? If not lemme know and I'll drop a little something on Rissa.

ATM

P.S. Oh yeah I got 34 stitches on my side, and one massive scar but Man's like Wolverine cuz. I'm healing up mad quick. They operated but said they had to leave the bullet in man. You see what these dudes have done. But its ite at least I can stand now. Once I can walk I'm leaving here. Stay up my darg. Good looking out.

Duane,

I just saw your Uncle Leroy. He was outside his favourite place.
The bookies that is, we spoke briefly. Even though we haven't been
on good terms and we can't agree, that's still my little brother. So I
had to show him some love. Anyway, your Uncle told me he's been
writing you and giving you 'man advice'! If that's true I'm glad to
hear he didn't forget about you.

My brother's no fool when he's ready, but when him drunk my
God, the foolishness that comes outta that man's mouth. Only God
knows, so don't pay him or his male philosophies too much mind,
you hear?

He told me he's been filling your head with his Mama Can't Raise
No Man theory. The same old theory me him and your Mum argued
about in 2000.

But he does makes some valid points. I know many sisters my age
who were left in a situation where they had to raise a boy pickney
by themselves. Of the few that I know I can't say whether they've all
become men if I'm honest. I'm no mental health nurse but a few of
them come across as a bit psychologically screwed. That might be
because of some of the tings the mothers were doing. I think you
and these young men of today probably do need that male nutrition
to become emotionally balanced men. Don't get me wrong it's the
same for us sisters, a women needs her father as well. If the roles
were switched I think a man would struggle in raising a girl child to
become a woman by himself, because chances are he wouldn't have
the right balance. Most men won't know many things about raising
a girl. He may not have the sensitivity or experience to express
certain things to a young girl child for example in relation to her
hormones.

It takes two to raise a man and two to raise a woman. And where I
come from it seem like we don't fight to keep our families together
any more. We don't give them the love and stability that they need.
Then we wanna sit down and wonder why our kids are always
failing at school or in and out of prison. Sorry but that's how I

feel and I'm not directing that at anyone I just mean that's us as a people.

But what is a man? First and foremost I think it's for a man to know himself, I think that's crucial as human beings, I think that's the first journey we should all be on. To know ourselves.

You can't tell anyone else about who to be if you don't know yourself. You can't pave the way for someone to be someone if you haven't walked the path yourself.

Forget the conditions of society, of culture, of race, screw all of that. It's about that journey within cos that's where all the answers are. And I know that nephew because I had to do it myself.

Aunty Jan-Jan

Bruv,

If you don't wanna leggo the road that's your business, but there comes a time when you stop doing this for the lifestyle and you have to reach a point where you're doing it for a greater purpose. Turn it around, get a house, a foundation for your future kids.

As a roadman everyday on road your only fear should be getting arrested. Nothing else matters, not beef, drama, nothing is worse than getting arrested and going to prison. That's the worse outcome. Every day you wake up, your only aim should be not to get arrested. Cos once they finally get you - which they will - your whole world's gonna crumble. Cos you don't know your sentence, how long you're gonna get, where you're going, you don't know what's gonna happen.

On the level ATM, when you were 14 I should've never given you half an ounce of my old line that was popping off. Yeah I taught you about getting money but I miss-taught you everything I thought I knew about manhood.

The roads are dead fam, too much drama. I remember me and the man dem use to laugh at dem man who was working in Primark, but when we see dem same man now, they're doing alright. So if they wanted to, they could laugh at man like me cos I've been in and out of jail and on pause for living the fast life while they're on road climbing the success ladder and enjoying their freedom. I'm not telling you to go look a job but this road ting ain't the one fam.

And don't think jail's brainwashed me to think the prison system works, cos it hasn't. They can judge me and punish me with time but they can't convince me my punishment was righteous, even if by law what I did was wrong. It's not even that cuz, I rehabilitate myself. So I can't keep looking back in time but I can look forward. You get me darg!

I know GTM's funeral is next week. If you feel like you gotta go then go. If you can't then cool don't force it. Whatever you do hurry up and get out of the endz.

Secretly though bruv, when my bredrin Cam got killed back in the day I wanted to ride out for him. I was ready to die for him. Then his Mum said I had better honour her son's memory. She said "why would you die for him when you can live for him?" That shit stuck with me forever.

Try better your life rude boy, don't waste another day.

Duane

Rissa,

You know what to tell you the truth I try not to think about what it's like being in here. Jail is jail, man just get on with it. You know how man stay already - we don't do the crying ting. Most man I know are detached from emotions. Well that's what I thought up until the other day.

I don't know what it is but recently I've been seeing bare man break down in 'ere. Certain man are breaking down in their cells cos they're doing a big bird or their missing their yutes but some of them go back on the wing and act hard again. It's only the other day I realised how much man in here are feeling the same pains. It's just that some of us are better trained at burying it. Man don't have no time for emotion. In here it's considered a weakness.

Nothing much to say about jail really, same shit different day. At 8 o'clock every morning the screws dem come wake man up. We come out our cells, choose what breakfast we want. Some man are tryna get a quick phone call in. You're not suppose to but some man will run over and dial a quick number, and when they get caught they'll be on some: "Come on Guv, 2 secs 2 secs quick tings" LOL. Then we jam in the cell for the rest of the morning, until lunchtime. We eat food in our cell.

A man might be in his cell all morning unless he's got education, or gym, or work or church/mosque. If you got those things you get let back out your cell and you'll hear a guvner scream out your name like: "Ricketts for education" or 'Whoever for Church.' Sometimes I wonder why certain youngers act so fascinated about jail life for.

Member the second time I come jail I went Brixton? Well Brixton was a mad one still, nuff man were in dere for violent offences. G-wing in Brixton was a greasy wing still, bare badman was in that wing. Everybody goes on one wing when they go to jail but you gotta work by behaving to go on a calmer behaved wing. Certain man don't know how to be easy. Dem kinna man are in here whiling out all the time and they don't make time in here any easier. The funny thing is dem same man can't even see why it's always hard for them. Oh yeah, then you get that wing for the fragiles, uno them man that get bullied. Nobody don't wanna go on that wing.

The first time I went jail I was working on server, which is basically working in the kitchen serving food, cleaning up and them type of things. When you do these things you get to come out of your cell more than the average person. The only man who don't come outta their cell too tuff, are those man who don't work or go worship or whatever. But most man do go gym. If you don't do anything you'd spend most of your day just literally locked up.

Certain man stay out of their cell all day, keeping busy.

After 6 o'clock man are allowed on the wing for an hour association which man call sosh. But everyone's cell is open and you can roam the wing. If there's no beef sosh can be bare joke for everyone but if there's beef brewing it can all kick off still.

In 'ere you got your North man wing, you're Sout man wing, East man wing and West man wing. It's that separated at times. If for example a man from East or wherever gets licked down on road and a man in jail see's his people are in a next wing shit can kick off. Even if they're on different wings, certain man will find a way to get onto a next wing to catch their enemy, whether he's bless with the screws dem or he's manipulating the screws dem, it's all politics in 'ere. If you're going gym or education you can easily buck a man from another endz cos they may be going gym or education too. If the wrong man see's you in the hallway shit can kick off. Other than that and sosh it's pretty much the exact same routine day in, day out.

If a beef kicks off it can cause a 24 hour lockdown. Then you can get a man whose vex with the man who got into beef for fucking up everyone's association, but that's how it goes. When an enemy does buck his enemy and it kicks off, they're more likely to get separated and put on different wings in the prison. Plus you get the next type of man who try bully up the place or rob dudes.

Man can go canteen, it's like going shop. Whenever I come back from canteen it's like I just come back from Tesco's sis LOL. Cos I proper stock up on my shit. It's not just me one though, certain man are in here having cell parties with their crisp and shit. I'm a man when I got tings and I see my people dem in 'ere I'll offer my peeps what I got, standard.

When I was in Brixton prison there was like 200 man on a wing and most of the mandem are black. True that's a black man jail, but Chelmsford, in Essex, that's more of a white man's jail.

When I was in Pents the screws dem move me off the Northtman wing cos I was having too much fun running joke with the mandem. This is jail sis and you can't let them see that you're comfortable. To make it harder for me they moved me to the Eastman wing. The fuckers don't like you getting too comfy so they left me to see how I would get on in them territories.

Lock up's 7oclock and that's it for the night. But if there's an emergency you can get out, for example if a man's bugging out and needs a breather he might get to speak to a listener. A listener is like an older person who has done a lot of bird and is still riding. I have to rate dem man talking positive, cos most of dem man ain't coming home for now.

In jail nobody don't know nothing unless you tell them – so if you're a man who's going block all the time no one ain't gonna know that

You can receive mail anytime in the day from 9-7 from the guvner. Either they throw it under your cell or if you're in association the guvner might just shout out: "Ricketts." Or whoever then you go to them and get your mail.

A man in jail can write a next man in jail if they put in a request. But you gotta know the guys first and second name, then they'll give you his prison number and he can write you back.

Certain screws deal with me ok still. One of them gave me some joke, he pulled me to a side one day on the wing and said: "You know what Ricketts, you're a good lad you are." lol

When a man's on basic it means he's riding it with the basics. No telly no nothing, you probably aint even got a kettle to make a cup of tea. Everyman starts on basic, and you gotta behave yourself to get your telly and come off basic. I don't care how bad a man is in here none of the mandem wanna ride basic. Especially when you can hear nuff man in their cell making bare noise cos there's a wicked film on, then you hear a man shout: "Oi fam did you see dat?" And you can't even relate to the rest of the mandem cos you're riding basic but every mans shouting through their window. A man might scream out: "Oi put it on channel 4 fam. Oi channel 5, channel 5." You can tell when everyman's watching the same film, from the reaction.

When Crimewatch is on a man might scream out to a next man on the landing! "Oi Ricketts, I just see you, you know fam. Your large, you're famous." Then a man will shout back: "Oi 'Llow me fam it wasn't me." One thing life's taught me is that no matter how hard it is you always gotta keep that sense of humour or you're finished sis. Sometimes man laugh so much I forgot I'm in prison. Until the jokes stop running and I'm sitting here thinking, beg someone else run a joke, keep the momentum lol.

Certain time it's not even the joke it could be the way it was said. I see Cockney man Jim from the Garage on my wing.

Cockney Jim's a man who makes himself at home in here. Jim was killing me with the joke yesterday. He was like: "Duane mate, it's lovely in here innit. I ain't gotta pay no rent, I can watch TV all day, I ain't got me wife nagging in me ears all day long. If you could see the man's face sis, the man was dead serious chatting bout: "All she fucking does is complain all day long I needed the fucking break from her". Cockney Jim had me dying in 'ere.

Then you get dem days that turn your stomach. Like when you here a man screaming out: "Stop, stop" or "I don't like it." Then you know some fuckery's going on. And it come like the whole jail goes quiet. And the next day no one won't even chat bout it.

When man's in jail you think about a lot of things you never think about on road. One time I sat down and was thinking so hard that I almost dropped a tear sis, and you know I don't cry easy. When you think too much in here, it can get like that.

Nothing ain't worse than the feeling when you get relaxed on a visit and forget that as soon as it started its almost done. It's the same feeling I get when I could only see the kids on the weekend, that feeling when they go is the worst feeling in the world.

Staring at this ceiling all evening gives you too much time to reflect. And by doing that I can see it all too clearly. Real talk sis, I get it now. I gotta lead by example. I gotta show Imarni that he don't have to go through the same things I have. I gotta show him love and teach him how to show love. As he's growing, I gotta teach him how to pick his Queen and to value her as he should. I gotta show Justice how to carry herself and to never settle.

Don't ask me about jail-life again please sis. It's not my favourite subject. I rather just do the time and not think about it. While I'm in here, I can't let my enemies see me down, so I keep on smiling. I hope my niece is O.K. Tell her Uncle said hello.

Duane X

Aunty Jan,

As a boy growing up I was confused by what my role was as a man. The outside world or society if you like taught me that as a man my role was to protect, more importantly I had to get cake, I mean provide. Truth be told Aunty J I'm tired of trying to explain what a man is. I just want to get out of here and see my yutes. So when you write me can you change the subject please?

Duane

Uncs wha gwarn?

I'm not even gonna lie to you Uncs your letters straight up kill me. It's like you're semi making sense one minute then you go somewhere else and completely lose me. One thing I can say about you Uncs is you're a man who ain't afraid to speak his mind.

And thanks for that score you sent, but why u always wasting ur money at the bookies? You proper love your Ladbrokes innit? That's your ting. Sometimes I imagine what you would be like if you dropped out the licar and dropped out the betting business. I wanna see the old you Uncs. Look how you lost 8 hundered in one day. If you keep fuckin with Ladbrokes your gonna end up a broke-lad. Trust me Uncs, I can't watch you go out like that.

What if your kids were to come back one day? What would you do? I know nuff men your age who walked out on their yutes. I hear the feminism argument you wrote me but that can't be every blackmans excuse. How long are you gonna make excuses for why you don't see your kids Uncs? And do you really wanna let them come back in your life and see you a broken man? Everyone one falls Unc but you gotta get back up man

You taught me that when I first came out of jail!

Keep ur head up Unc aka Drunken Master.

Peace
Duane

Duane,

I went to the hospital twice this week. First time to drop the letter you sent, and secondly to pick up any letter he had for you. But when I went there they said Anton's discharged himself. No one has seen him bro...

Rissa

Thanks Sis,

It's cool maybe it's a good thing. Maybe ATM took my advice and went country. That's good cos I thought he was gonna stay and do a mad one.

Anyway I hate to ask you sis, man pride and that, but have you got a score you can borrow me? I've been kinda short lately. I can't ask Redz, I don't wanna take the piss. Redz has posted more than enough P through your door for me already.

Duane

Yeah I got you bro,

I did notice Redz hasn't posted anything lately. Was planning to send you some change anyway, please don't let pride get in between me and you. You know if I've got it, I'll help.

It was interesting to read that letter about how you're living in there. Obviously I slyly miss you and I've always wondered why you choose to live the life you live. I don't know what it's like to have a certain mindset or to feel like pride is the only thing you have. I guess don't know what it's like to feel disrespected from a man's point of view.

I won't say I know what it's like to be a man. And I'm not saying the system doesn't make it harder for brothers or working class men of any shade to work within the system. What I'm saying is the working class man and the black man should have more strength not to fall into the traps that are created. If you men had better role models who were accessible, on a constant basis, maybe things would be different.

For example, look at you bro. You've got the twins now bruv, and you've learnt things the hard way. But because of you changing your son is unlikely to make the same mistakes that you've made cos you'll always be around to show him different. It's good you're trying to change in time to show him the traps. Unlike our wasteman of a puppa. I honestly don't know why you would contemplate letting him back in your life. He ain't no role model to you, you're a role model to him.

Bruv, I might not have told you this before, but I look at you as a man with a lot of potential who's not tapping into it. And it feels like I have an addict as a brother, because you're trapped in a cycle that's giving you some type of buzz or some type of reassurance of your manhood. It's become normal to you cos you've been in the cycle for so long. Trust me I wish I could take you out of it Duane but until you hit your rock bottom it's like your life will always revolve around the streets. It's the company you keep. No matter how much I do as a sister, I can't pull you out of it.

The only way you're gonna get out of it is when you see it for yourself. I can't get into your head, I can't get it across to you! So as your sister I feel helpless. It cripples me, because I love you and I wanna help you, and I wanna show you a better quality of life

Mum did the best she could to raise us. And you just treat her like she's invisible. I know she ain't perfect Duane but she did her best innit. To go jail 3 times before 25 must mean you're doing something wrong. You can't keep on making excuses bruv. Sorry for the rant but it's been weighing on my heart. And you know I'm always gonna speak my mind.

Please try and stay out of trouble so you can come home early on tag, that would be good. Your niece misses her Uncle. Love you bruh.

Rissa

Aunty J,

You know mum always taught me as a black man I have to work ten times harder but I wonder, even if I wasn't a black man, would I still have to work ten times harder to figure out what manhood is as a fatherless child?! Because there's levels to this shit.

Just a random thought I was having. Hope you had a good week AJ

Duane

Lickle Nephew,

U think ur the man sometimes don't you? And it come like ur forgetting yourself too. True you're doing your little road ting you wanna try look down pon your uncle Leroy. Well hear wot rude boy I don't care what money u made outta road back in your day, or who rates u in jail. When u write me you better come correct bredrin. This same man ur chatting to like some waste man use to clean ur waste. That's right u renking lickle pussyface you. Who d'you think it was that use to clean ur do-do nappy dem when ur Mum went to college and needed a child minder? Me! - now u wanna try run up your gums like you're the Uncle. You stay there rude-boy with ur little willie! Done the talk cos I'm too drunk - I mean too tired to cuss and write right now. Further more send me a VO since ur such a badman now, and see if I don't come and bust ur rarse. Try me, and see how fast ill come and tump u in ur face in front of da screws and all ah ur little Bredrin dem. Its only true ur my little sistas child why I ain't touch u yet, u better try know.

Tell me Sutten

What makes u a better man than me?

Alright, alrite cussing aside now nephew, you don't know what you think you know yunah. You cyan't diss all the fathers dem from my generation, chat bout excuses. You don't know the full story bredrin. You think it's just feminism why the fathers fucked off? Nah dred.

Listen me good bredrin nuff men Inna my time was laying round with gyal doing their business with no real commitment and no intention of having any yutes with the women they were laying down with. More-time the brudder just met the girl last week, having fun going out there getting his dirty on. Then a gyal wanna turn around and say to him I'm pregnant. Listen Dred, in my time man don't wanna hear dem fuckery. Cos when we was doing the dirty, more-time a girl would tell you say she's taking this protection, doing this or whatever the case may be. And us man are so fool we believed that. Then she gets pregnant and tells you what she's doing with your baby. Without considering a rarse about what you feel.

But these times bredrin, she aint even met your parents, she don't even know where you live dred.

So what, she don't know not one of my friend dem and she's bawling she's pregnant for me? What you talking about? Man aint no eeediat, what because she wants that flat? And now she's gonna go around and tell the world about how wutless I am? And how I don't wanna look after my pickney? What the rarse? So many man my age had my kinda attitude nephew.

Then you got another man he's got green eyes – poor ting, poor ting. And worse still he's red skin. Oh My GOD. He's finished. If the man all sit down next to a woman she breed for him... poor ting.

And then he's a wutless farder cos he don't wanna check his yute. But she pre-planned it cos his eyes and his curly hair. And she never thought in a million years that he wouldn't stay. But she never did her research on him. He's a gyalist and he's a roadman that's everywhere, he gets about. You can find him uppa Manchester, Birmingham, all Brixton, Harlesdan Tottenham Hackney, he's everywhere, like I said he's a gyalist. Him just ah stick and move. And if a girl tries it with him he'll 'av some of dat cos he's a coxman. He's known for dat. He was dead for gyal in school, him never get nothing back then, but now he feels good for being a gyalist. Dem kinna man 'av got yutes all over the place bredrin. People know him as dirty Trevor, man like Trevor's never been seen with no h'ugly gyal to date. But real talk the man Trevor was a target cos of his eyes, hair and complexion. You'd be surprised mi nephew the tings that did happen in my time kmt. Then a woman wanna turn round and tell her boy pickney say his Daddy isn't a real man kmt.

Anyway dred you dissed me. Chat bout, I should put down the drink and left the bookies alone. Kmt. I dun tell you why I drink already bredrin. And fuck Babylon I don't want no 9-5, a job is short for 'just over broke'. I refuse to work for Babylon dred. I don't beg them for nothing. My parent's generation come here and help dem win World War 2 and they still treat man fuckery. Yeah they gimme ah lickle housing benefit when time I got my flat. Other than that I make my own money dred. Like a real man.

I drink more than the average man yes. But who Jah bless no man curse. You think I don't know the family chat about me and about how I'm a gambling addict bredrin? Yeah I dun know that already, but I don't business. The way I see it, I'm an entrepreneur. I'm a man who can make decisions under pressure. I don't answer to no man; I'm like a self employed investor. Oh and what's the difference between us Mr BIG shot? You smoke your weed when you're stressed, I like my Wray when I'm vex. You're addicted to the hustle on the street, I'm addicted to the hustle in the local bookies. So you tell me what's so different?

Kmt. You diss mi bad mi nephew, you gone too farrr now! Your lucky you're Audrey's pickney, I'm telling you. If you wasn't I woulda straight bruck it up bredrin....

Uncle Leeroy

P.S. Facety little rarseklart...

KMT

Duane,

When you black boys are growing up, you're constantly being told or are told at least once, that life is gonna be more difficult for you because you're a black male. For me nephew telling your son his life's gonna be difficult can't be positive. By telling them that they're going to be oppressed, or they're going to be rejected or they're going to find life difficult, can't be a good thing. How can you expect a child to feel good about himself if he's taught he has to work ten times harder in life?!

I don't think that that's a very good strategy for raising black boys. Cos a child wants to know that they are of value, that they are of worth, that they are someone, that they will be someone. They want to have a positive sense of self and identity.

I read your letters and take on some of what you say about being a man. I just think it's always gonna be difficult for a man because you guys don't always know yourselves.

Some men believe that to have sex makes them a man. There is a pressure to become that type of man in this day and age. For a boy becoming a man having sex for the first time is like saying, I have arrived.

Imagine I was on the bus coming home from work yesterday when I overheard these two boys speaking. One of them said: "Bruv! Would you beat the girl that you first did it with?" And the fact that they called it beating made me feel some kind of way. Then the other boy said: "Nah bruv she's dead, I wouldn't go anywhere near her now."

The way he said it - beating, I mean I've heard other descriptions like fucking. But beating is such a brutal term. And that made me see how you young men value and learn about women and sex.

For any man to be who he truly is, he has to know love and how to love. And a lot of you men aren't men because you don't know love and can't give love. Some of us really underestimate the value of being taught love. And a lot of you men out there didn't know what it was like to get a hug on the breast of reassurance. A lot of men haven't got the right foundations there.

You need Love.

I'm talking 'bout that love that don't discriminate, that love that's always there. That love that has strength. Love! Genuine love, old skool love, that's what I'm talking about. A lot of people don't know what that is.

Children don't stop and start growing when it suits the parent. It's continuous. It's organic. Yuh understand? And a lot of people don't understand what the soul is, what the spirit is. People don't understand what love is. They don't know how to nurture that. Nurture the spirit so that a human being can become total. When you become total you can deal with anything.

Aunty Jan

Aunty Jan,

You know mum taught me from young not to lay round with different women? She said every time you lay down with a girl "you lose a piece of you." That use to spook me out so I buried that thought in the back of my mind but she was right.

I heard you in your other letter about being positive and that. Trust me AJ, I'm really trying to take note but earlier today one dude tried to start some drama. He was in the last prison with me and we both got shipped to Swaleside together, he's been getting on my nerves for a little while now. Today I walked away but I feel like he's going to draw me out. It will only be a matter of time before I have to do my ting. It's like the more man in here see I'm trying to be positive, the more they wanna try it. Man in here have a way of taking this kindness for weakness and if they carry on I'm gonna be forced to weaken my kindness. I'm not taking any shit from no-one. You see when you're in a place like this aunty you can't really be yourself more time. So there ain't much time to love yourself. In here you gotta protect yourself first.

Anyway take care for now AJ.

Duane

Nephew,

What foolishness are you talking? You better fin' time to love yourself before you ruin any chances you have of coming out of that place with all your faculties.

So you got a problem brewing and you might need to defend yourself? Fine, that's survival. I get that but what energy are you attracting while you're in there? What energy are you giving off to these guys testing you? I get that you are in a very hostile environment, I get that. And to survive, well, I guess you're gonna have to do what you have to do.

We Ricketts don't live by fear but I feel like you're always living in fear, and I don't mean fear as in you're afraid of people. I mean, as in your mindset is in constant fear that you have to be ready to rock, ready to fight. I tell you what son that's not good for you psychologically or emotionally.

This is where things like faith come in, you have to walk in faith. You have to know the most high is protecting you, walk in peace. Don't fear anyone around you.

Obviously in a real battle situation you have to be physically ready. Go gym, stay strong but mentally you must walk in peace because sometimes our energies create more drama for us. Try it. And I know this might sound crazy but sometimes you have to just take a beating cos you know you're getting out. You know you're gonna be good. You can't keep doing people damage in self-defence cos it's only you getting extra time for that.

I don't know what's wrong with the mentality some of you men have. All I know is if you want to be at peace in there, when you see your brother you got to see yourself.
Love you neph.

Stay tuned

AJ x

Bro,

It's been a minute, I hope your good.

Why is it when you brothers got a good girl at home who will hold you down you treat them bad? She might not be perfect no one is, you might think she's a bit of drama sometimes, but why don't you lot try hold her down and work with her? Work through your issues.

I just feel like our generation are getting into some here and now relationships and not looking at what it really is. It's about the longevity. More so when you're having kids. That's like a step into marriage really, not saying you have to get married overnight but you are a family now, get to grips with that. If you're gonna be bringing a life in the world, I think you gotta try to have a lifelong relationship with that person. And it's like everyone wants everyone to be perfect – I don't want her to argue, I don't want him to do this or that. I mean, really?!

You young parents should try sitting down with people that have been together 20 odd years. And ask them what they've gone through, what they've had to put up with. Their ups and downs. Elaborate on what the real reasons are for why men always cheat when they got a good woman? Let me know, I wanna hear it... Kevin said he left me for some next skinny white girl because black girls are too much headache.

You can leave a black girl to go with a white girl or vice versa, you still got responsibilities to that girl. You're still gonna have arguments. It might not be so intense but it's still headache innit. I don't care what you say, in my opinion 99.9% of men are dogs.

Stay well bro.

Teah x

Aunty Jan,

You say when I look at my brother I need to see myself and I hear all of dat, but it don't work. Cos when it gets peak in here and that same so called brother is on the landing screw facing me with all his facial muscles, you best believe he doesn't see himself in me. He sees me the same way the rest of the world does — as a threat. In this concrete jungle someone's always gonna be the prey and that someone's not me. How d'you expect me to see a man as my brother when he sees me the way he does? Really AJ I don't think your method is gonna work for me in here.

You see in this place aunty if a man don't know who you are and they think they can, they will try and test you, to see if you're on it. I've still got that guy I told you about before trying to test me, it's like it never stops.

I do hear what you're saying though. I do read back over your letters and I think to an extent you do understand manhood but u don't overstand it. I can't have no time for emotion for many a reason. Remember one thing, I'm a bruva from the roads and the madness I go through is a combination of the streets and other things. And that's why I don't tap into my emotions like that. But you wouldn't understand that side to it. You've never been a brother and you've never been on the roads (or prison) so your version of manhood and mine will never be in line. Can we change the subject please? Love AJ

Duane x

Duane,

It makes me so sad to hear about the harsh surroundings you're in right now. You're right I'm not from no street but neither are you. My sister raised your backside in a home. You might have spent a lot of your time on the street or in prison, so for that I overstand the streets is a big part of your life and where your understanding comes from. But don't you ever diss my sister Audrey by saying you're from the streets. I don't need to be from road to see that you got the street rules and the home rules confused.

It can't be easy for you, I overstand that too. But your kids and partner need to see you treat them better than the people in the concrete jungle that mean you harm. Your family at home love you. Stop being so angry with life so you can receive that love and give it back when you step in the home. Remember the streets is how you once lived, it's not who you are. Know yourself.

Aunty Jan-Jan

Teah,

First of all your boy Kevin's a doughnut. Man who put down sisters are a waste of space.

And how you still chatting all this, all mandem are dog talk? Leave it out luv LOL. I hope I'm in that 00.1% of real men.

Real talk though you can't judge all men as dogs unless you see the way they've grown up. Things that they've learnt or mislearnt to be appropriate behaviour.

Sometimes you chat like you didn't grow up in the same estate as me.

As a man growing up on the farm, you think you can say no to a girl if she wants you? You must be crazy, and live where? If a girl offered a brother da beat back then and he turns that down, he's done for, he would never hear the end of it.

Remember, we use to have keys to this pitch black abandon flat on the estate? All the mandem would be up in the yard jamming. Then when a man brings back a link with him, he automatically gets the key to the flat. No C-blocking is allowed. Every other man inside has to go chill outside until a brother's finished doing his ting.

The mandem would still be cotchin' outside running joke, waiting for a brother to finish. If a man came out too quick, a next man would crack joke and say look how quick he was. You're a one hit wonder. Or she weren't even making no noise; you got a small one lol. Men are under pressure, so we feel the need to go build up some confidence. And confidence comes with experience. So a young boy may lay down with a few girls, before he first settles down. Because in his mind a man can't be with a girl he really likes if he's not sure that he's good at what he's doing. Peer pressure's a bitch growing up in the hood. You've seen American Pie right? Well, the mandem was hungy for gyal from young. We coulda made our own film and called that shit English Saltfish Pattie.

Moretime we've been taught better ways of manhood, but we picked up a next version of it as we grew. Unfortunately, the form of manhood we picked up wasn't always a good example.

I remember when we was in year 7. I must of had one girlfriend at the time. Me and her was going strong still, y'know puppy love and all that. All up to summer holidays me and this girl is still boyfriend and girlfriend. Anyway I'm there chilling at one youth centre, and people coming up to me telling me some next girl likes me innit. So I was like: "Nah nah nah I've already gotta girl and what not." The mandem were looking at me like I was mad lol. One brudder kept looking at me like: Are you stuuupid? Bruv, don't say nothing to your girl she don't need to know. At that age they made me feel some kinda way, like something was wrong with me. And real talk from then on, any girl I got with after that, I never took loyalty as a normal part of a relationship.

As I got older I saw and mis-learnt more things that let me know I wasn't meant to have just one girl. Imagine one time in year 8, I must of had some girls at my house who were just my bredrins, you was there aswell Teah. After I walked yous lot to the bus stop, and came back from the bus stop I saw couple of the older girls on the estate grinning teet. And they was like: "Gwarn Duane, ah you dat!" gyal dem Kit-Kat, gwarn rudeboy." Lol So basically I was getting bigged up, gassed up, for having 3 female friends in my yard who were genuinely just friends. What do you think a young man learns by that?

Even sex itself. As boys we were mis-taught about the concept of sex. As a yute I've overheard plenty grown women chat bout they don't want no one-minute man. That gives a young boy a certain pressure to live up to. From 12/13 guess what us man were doing? We were on road trying to link bigger gyal like 16 plus. Cos that way, if you beat a girl at that age and don't hear no complaints, then your sex game can't be dead lol. So we lie to them older girls and say that we're 16 when we're only 12/13, but that's what it was, it's a man ting Teah.

Real talk though, nuff man don't like rejection from their gyal una. It makes them feel some kinda way. No man wants to be with a gyal that hits him regularly with that: "I'm not in the mood for it today." That ration talk can make a brudder feel inadequate. He might start thinking he's lost his touch. And they say the devil makes work for idle hands. You can't make a man think he's not good enough, or you're getting bored with him. Cah he won't tell you - he'll just go and build his confidence back up. And like my Uncle says 'no man don't want any sympathy pum-pum.' Lol. But he's right in a sense. No man wants love out of pity. He might take it cos some man are like that. But he will know it weren't 100.

I've had to fight to adjust a lot of my old ways. I've been in constant conflict with self. I had to let go of being a man in the world that I come from, to being a man in the right way that Candy and the twins needed. And somehow I still fell short. All I'm saying to you is that journey from boy to manhood ain't a straight road.

Holla back sis.

Duane

Marissa,

You keep going on about Mum and how I deal with her. I can only deal with Mum the way she deals with me. I show Mum love the way she shows me.

Remember when I got shot Mum couldn't even bring herself to hug me out of trying to teach me a certain strength. And that's how it is for me in and out of jail, man have to always be hard. You can't put your guard down, so you can never be yourself.

I can't believe you think I'm a street addict LOL. But you're right about one thing, my circle, that shits changing as we speak. Understand I've spent more time with that circle on road and in jail than I have with my own family. We don't only have a family inside the home, we have one outside the home too.

I wouldn't agree I'm a street addict I use to be glued to that way of thinking but not so much now. I'm not playing victim, I'm not saying I was forced to go on the roads. Everyone's got a choice innit. I had a choice, just like everyone else does. All I'm saying is the reason why I chose what I chose at age 14 is because of what I saw around me as a boy growing up.

My definition of manhood at that age was someone who doesn't need anything from anyone. A man was someone who's driving a car because a man needs his freedom. A man had to have money cos he needed to be able to buy what he wants, do what he wants, go where he wants, all of that, that was my definition of a man when I was growing up. So that's what I was striving towards, having money, having clothes having transport, all that material stuff. Being able to not have to ask Mum, who couldn't afford it.

It's long writing Riss, certain tings I don't expect you to understand. Glad to know you see my potential – means a lot sis.

Duane x

AJ,

I hear you but tell me if you see where I'm coming from as a man.
Before my child was born I remember the mother of my children's
mother going on and on in ma head saying: "You better not cheat
on ma daughter." Over and over again. And if I'm honest that shit
wasn't motivational for me, it kinda left a dent in the way I was
being viewed by her family, I kinda knew I wasn't welcome I felt like
the hood guy who breeded their daughter. They almost gave the
impression like I wasn't good enough for Candy. Like I fucked up
her future. Like they were forced in to putting on a temporary act
while they waited for me to slip up.

When my children were born I felt like I was pushed out of
everything. I thought I would be able to get some one on one time
with them. I thought I would finally get to bond with these beautiful
twins that were arriving, to find myself as a father. But to be honest,
it wasn't what I expected from the time my girl was in labour. I tried
to comfort her through the birth but she only seemed to want her
mother's support. It's like she didn't need me. Then when it was
time to go home, my girl's sister Lorna came to pick up my children
with the car seats and wanted to be the one to carry my child
outta the hospital. I was baffled. I mean I wanted to carry my own
child along with the mother carrying the other twin.

I was supposed to be the protector.

I actually had to take my own newborn child out of my girl's sister's
hands. Maddest thing is if I didn't make a big deal, my girl would've
been cool to just let her sister do that shit. At first I thought maybe
I was just being over the top, and overprotective but the bottom
line is, that's my natural instinct as a man and as a father, to protect
my family.

As soon as we got back to her Mum's yard it was all about my girl
and the twins, which was cool at first, I understood. Then it got
overwhelming. A brother was starting to feel invisible. So I just
started thinking, fuck this, what is my role?

Mama Can't Raise No Man

I got so tired of fighting for my position that I switched off. I switched off my emotions to my children or the joy of being a father cos I felt like I had it taken from me. The role should've been mine; I got both the nurturing role taken from me and the protecting role taken from me.

So what I did was I kept it all to myself cos men ain't meant to complain. I just took the back seat that was given to me and turned my attention to making money. So in that sense I learned to emotionally detach myself from something where I didn't feel there was any space for me.

In this day and age, I feel like sometimes men just ain't respected. We always gotta fight to be recognised, espepcially within the family role and that can't be right. Often a mother who needs help is able to better provide for the child via support from the government then the support of the father of their child. So I can see why a mother mght feel like she needs to wear the crown of the king as well as the queen. They're in a position to lead and provide and able to do it on their own. But the result is that as a man you don't feel like a King and so find it hard to act like one.

I guess what I'm saying AJ is that I don't know how to be the King, ya feel me? Love AJ.

Duane

Duane,

If I'm totally honest with you, I'm guilty of that same thing – thinking I was the man in my family. Cos when I was growing up I saw domestic violence in my house. So coming from a family with two girls we learned to put our foot down, and of course your Uncle Leroy was the baby so he didn't have much of a say. Seeing guys beat up on mum just made me gain that independent attitude and promise myself that when I got older, none of this shit was gonna happen to me. My mudder would tell me don't ever let no man treat you like a doormat.

I understand why you young guys don't always feel like you have a place in the house or family. Sometimes women are too independent. We don't always respect or show respect for the role our partners play and have. I can see how this can be very damaging for the whole family. Maybe especially for young women who may then do the same in their relationships as they have their own families. I guess us woman needs to be more nurturing to our men to help them develop. We sometimes forget about all that hurt a man has had to hold in because he's not been taught or allowed to express himself as a man. Maybe it's true that we don't give enough understanding when it comes to a man's experience of having to deal with the roads.

You know me and Patrick have been married going on 20 years now. And when the boys were getting older they would come home and say someone had hit them at school or outside. And every time Patrick would tell the boys to go tump them down. He was always telling the boys if someone hits them, they must hit them back. Me and Patrick use to have constant arguments about that. I was always quick to challenge him with what he should be doing with the boys. Saying you can't do this, you can't do that. Then one time Patrick got vex and turned to me and said to me: "Well what do you want me to do woman?" And that's kinda when I realised how controlling I was being.

Duane, stop being so damn hard on yourself and that beautiful ex- missus of yours. She's just like you. Young and doing the best that she can. Learn to let things go. You both need to stop putting so much on each other. You guys need to be the best you can be according to your ability. No one knows your (flight/plight) like you. You can tell me all you want but I'll never fully understand where you're coming from because I haven't lived it. The only person that truly understands is you. So you need to become one with yourself.

You know I only cuss at you because I love you. So take no offence. Has everything calmed down with the guy you had tension with?

Aunty Jan X

Aunty Jan,

Not really. One of his friends started running up his mouth in association so I just flipped and said: "Who the fuck you talking to rudebwoy? You think you're the only one in here that's somebody? I'm somebody too y'nah ask about me Ricketts!!! Behave yourself" I could sense that when I said that some of his own boys kinda agreed. Cos this brudders one of them man who just over feels themselves. He's a troublemaker. Only cos he's got bare soldiers round him and a portion of muscles. And man know he's in there for murder. He's just big headed cos everyone in here knows him and he's got a rep where everyman in the prison bigs him up when they walk past him. But you know me Aunty Jan I don't really care who you are or what you've done. That's your business until you start trying to disrespect me.

Anyway, it's all good. This is just part of prison life.
Love Aunty J

Duane

D,

I'm not against you, remember that. And I hear what you're saying but what do you want from me? Ever since the first time you went to prison and got shot you've been telling me all of the things that you're frustrated about. And I'm always here trying to help you and even with all the effort I put into trying to help, you're still frustrated. So what do you want from me? I'm looking at you like your sick, you're an addict in my eyes and the roads are your drug. This is all you know, it's what makes you feel like a man. And as long as you're feeling like a man, that's your high. So who am I to tell you any different kmt!

Riss

Riss,

Real talk, you're right. I apologise if I sound like I was coming at you in some kind ah way. I'm just pissed being in here for something I didn't even do. I don't know what I want from you. I was just venting cos I'm mad frustrated. How can I find the answers if I don't know the questions? I've tried to make you understand the life I've lived but it's long. I can't expect you to know where I'm coming from if it took me this long to figure it out myself. I'm done talking bout it sis, you'll never get where man's coming from. How could you?!

Let's just leave it as that. It's all love.

Duane

Teah,

I'm glad you asked how long us man are gonna use dem same dead excuses for? Well T, all I can do is talk for me and I'm trying to change for real this time. I'm not even with Candy and I'm still acting like I'm not single. I'm in here getting anonymous letters from half naked girls writing me and for once I'm not entertaining it.

I don't condone the cheating I did and am sorry for it. Cos if I say to a girl I love her, I gotta learn to respect her innit. Deep down I always knew better but I just didn't know how to apply better. I'm learning to do that the more I grow; I'm tryna work on how to express and receive love. Cos a world without love can be a cold cold world.

What gets me mad though is how a girl would ask you why you cheated and when you give her the reason, she doesn't even try to understand, she'll just call it an excuse. Life's about learning and learning is never complete but as far as Candy and her big forehead sister see it, Duane's forever wrong innit.

When Candy first kicked me out I was feeling so cold I was ready to turn my back on the world forever. But that cold feeling didn't last and I returned after a few months. I realised my yutes were more important than the hurt I was feeling at the time. And that if I reject them cos I feel rejected then I'm no better than man who rejected me.

I'll never walk out on my yutes T, I just needed that time to get my head clear. Women hurt men daily. A woman can break a man's heart by just not believing in him. That alone fam.

Another thing, why is it a girl will say some dumb shit like: "If men can cheat and be forgiven then it should be ok for us to do the same thing? And when you tell a girl it's not the same thing she thinks you're being a hypocrite. But it's not the same thing we were raised fucking different. You was taught to be a lady and keep your legs closed and us man dem were taught to open them. There's no way you should make the same mistakes as me. Or pick up our nasty habits to prove a point

So yeah, if the shoe was on the other foot and Candy cheated, man would've left her. Call me a hypocrite all you want.

Real talk Teah, from here on Candy can link whomever she wants from wherever she wants. Man don't care 'bout all that. My only care is the twins. Candy can move on if she wants as long as she ain't bringing no roadman or funny don round my yutes, it's fine.

When she finds this next fella she'll be convinced she's found an upgrade. But if he is good to her how can she be sure that he didn't learn the error of his ways by breaking some next poor girl's heart? People like to compare relationships, but unless the fella she's linking is 16 years old, she can't compare us. From boy to man.

Sometimes T, I wish that I knew then what I know now. But they do say when you know better, you can do better!

I hope you get that job you applied for. You're making big moves sis.

Duane

Wha gwarn my darg?

Been a couple months still. Man just lan' back in the country. I flew out to Cyprus for a quick holiday. Just felt I had to get away and clear my head for a week. I heard about your youngers dem, I told you this would happen. Imagine G.T.M use to work for me now he's dead – crazy. I heard they didn't want him, that they actually come for your boy A.T.M .

Anyway G, when I was out there on the beach I was thinking hard about life and back in the day. I knew the block didn't have love for man from the first time I got locked up. I realised it's everyman for himself. It was only you out of all of the man dem who came on a visit. Only you wrote man letters. Only you went to check on Marjay for me, the rest of the mandem are flakey. It's only you, who has my back when shit hits the fan. I always told you M.O.E aint nothing without us, dem man are plastic, they aint built like us.

I thought I'd let you know I've decided to forget I had a yute with that bitch Selina and just get on with my new life. It might sound fucked but if I don't move on, this shit's gonna send me mad, you know how it go already.

Selina can do what she wants. She can change Malik's school, or leave the effing country if she likes, I won't waste my time running her down no more. Sometimes I think about how sad it is that Malik will never know what efforts I've made to see him before I decided to give up.

I've done everything to see my yute. From hiding outside his school like some stalker just to get a glimpse, to waiting near the bus stop they usually take home. I've even gone to the mum's yard to find out where my yute is but I don't think she's really bothered. True her man bussed out on her and her yute, she don't give a damn. Nuff time I've seen kids that resemble mine when I'm going down the road and it just fucks my head up. Or when my bredrins are around me with their yutes, that does my head in cah obviously I can't see mine grow.

One time I wanted to go grab Malik from his school. But when I really checked it I knew it didn't make sense cos if I go and grab him I'm only gonna catch another charge. And I told you I'm not ever going back to jail. Some of these girls are lost fam. They proper go out buying themselves fathers days cards, its mental lol.

I see my bad mind baby mother Selina in Brown Eagle last week. I told her I wanna see my kid. Hear what the bitch told me, she said it's up to the judge to decide! That's why I'm like fuck it she can just keep him. I'm done. I'm only taking care of Caprice from here onwards.

Anyway my darg. Fuck everyone, it's just about getting paper (legitly). When you come out I got you don't stress nothing M.O.E Money Over Everyting.

Redz

Redz,

Why the fuck am I hearing that the rumour about you and Rueben aint a rumour?

My new cellmate told me how you tried to set up Rueben. Why the fuck would you try set up one of the mandem for? One of our own bredrins? A man told me you gave him Rueben's mums address back in the day so him and his bredrins from South could rob him. Why the fuck would you do that? What cos Rueben was shining and getting attention in the hood you felt you had to dim his light? All this time you was making out Rueben was hating on you, when all along it was you hating on him. You lied bruv and you lied to get me to think Ruebs and the mandem hated me too.

When I first heard rumour from Rueben's twin brother Byron that you snaked Rueben, I didn't wanna believe it. The last time I was on road and you was locked up I spoke to you and you said it weren't true and that whoever's saying that is trying to mess up the fam.

Byron and Rueben were gonna lick your head off and I fell out with dem man I grew up with cos I defended your name. I even switched on ATM when he was trying to show me who you really are. But now I'm sitting in here with the same sed brudder who said you gave him the address and told him to peel Rueben. So first I hear you're a snitch, now mans seeing live proof you snaked one of your own people for paper. I can't defend a man who's a snake so tell me sutten different, tell me it ain't so darg!

Duane

Yo darg wha gwan?

Why you coming at me like that in your letter? All aggressive and shit. Alright you wanna know the truth yeah. Fuck it then, I did do it! Fuck Reuben too! Reuben snaked me, about I snaked Rueben. How can I be the snake when it was me who brung Rueben on this trapping game? Who do you think it was that had to back Reuben in school when the turks use to bully him – ME! So how could I be the snake. Before me Reuben was just some any lightskin boy.

How can I be the snake darg, how? This same yute Rueben never sent me no money when I was in jail. Fuck Rueben and his brother. They saw me the other day and weren't saying nutten, dem man aint licking off no ones head – they're all talk.

You shouldn't listen to rumours, but since we're on the subject I might as well talk up da tings. I do kinda work with boydem but I'm not no snitch. Let's just say I can get you out on early release tag if you wanna do the same line of work. The people I work with know about the relationship you have with the yutes on the streets as a youth worker and they said they could use a guy like you on the team. I told them you're like me and they said to offer you the chance to make the jump. Fuck the hood D. Imagine us both getting out the hood just by working with the old bill. We can make P's fam and move outta Totty forever. Man could go clear.

M.O.E 4 Life.

Redz

Redz,

What fuckery are you on? I never knew you were a funny don like this. So you're just gonna sit there and try justify the fact that you tried to set up Reuben? He was supposed to be your friend. If this is how you treat your friends, I don't even wanna know how you treat your enemies. Are you for real? And to make it worse you're tryna offer me early release and a job working alongside feds, are you ok? Is this what you thought us man meant when we said M.O.E (Money Over Everything?) You know who you're talking to? I beg you miss me with that shit. I'd rather be a voluntary lollipop man than work with the feds in any capacity.

I dunno who you are any more Redz, who the fuck are you? Stop letting trees die in vein by chatting shit on paper.

Duane

Duane,

You're right, you're so right. I will never understand where you're coming from. As long as your fight is to get me to understand, you will always be frustrated with me. My path and your path are two different paths. I've never lived your life. I've never walked in your shoes, so I'll never understand. It's just like me telling you about what I have to face as a woman and expecting you to understand.

I feel sad for you because I know your situation and I want better for you. I recognise that as a black man growing up where and how you did, you have to deal with certain things as standard. I don't get stopped and searched. I'm not living with the constant risk of getting stabbed or shot. I don't have to choose between the path of friends before me or trying to make it standing on my ones as a lone solider and going against the grain. I don't face the constant possibility of being in and out of jail because of a lifestyle that's hard to escape from.

So rather than me trying to feel your pain, just let me be that voice to encourage you and empower you to do what you need to do.

Teah x

Yo my brudda,

Ahh man you're gonna be pissed. I know what you're gonna say already darg.

Man got caught with the burner sitting outside the yutes yard. The yutes who rubbed out my boy I mean. Police jumped out on me and shift man. I tried to run but obviously my rib ain't healed up proper yet. As you can see from the top of the letter I'm in jail now, I'm on remand cuz. Ahhh sorry G, man knows he fucked up.

Man just felt pissed. I heard dem man who duppied GTM were sitting on mad paper. I was looking to peel dem quickly, to even tings up then go country and kick-back today. I'm pissed bruv I can't even send you no money again.

They got me here in Thameside bruv. I can't lie it's kinda ite in here. I got phone in my cell and it's newish. But I'm getting shipped out soon cos I kicked off with some big man who said I rushed his son.

Man shoulda listened when you told me to seckle down but fuck it, whatever happens, happens.

Sorry if I let you down bro. It just is what it is. And you know how it go already.

ATM

ATM,

I'm not your Dad bruv don't say sorry to me, apologise to yourself.
Pissed? I'm more than pissed bruv, I'm wounded by that news. I all
ripped the letter up I was that vex. Then I asked myself why am I so
vex? And it's cos I thought one day the penny would drop. That you
would get all what I was trying to say to you. Now I'm sitting here
pissed with a pen in my hand trying not to write the words - I told
you so.

So, what you saying now? You mean to tell me all this time you were
the one keeping it 100 sending me money? And the dutty glory
hunter Redz was taking the credit what a litte P......

Say no more, its cool, imma handle this. Good looking out though,
try know I appreciate that. And my bad for not hearing your
warning – my eyes were closed

I guess you could say you told me so too little bro.
Write me when they ship you out. High chance they'll send you
Swaleside so we might see each other sooner than you think. Until
then walk safe G.

Duane

P.S. Don't bring no hype ting to jail fam. This ain't the arena.

Duane,

Sorry you haven't got a response from me for almost 2 months. Just dealing with some personal issues, you know how life go.

Anyway back to what you wrote me. I hear you son, sorry I mean Duane, I hear you. So confirmation of manhood is what you needed from me! I see your point, I fully do. Not sure if I fully agree with all you said but I see your point.

Just one question: if you don't mind! Let's say Errol stayed around. What makes you think I would have been a good enough example to you of what a man is? Where would you have got your confirmation of manhood from if I stayed and was a bad example of a man?
You see all I'm saying is you Marrissa and your Mum might have all been better off without me for all we know.

Maybe you have a point when you say you learnt manhood from the streets but this doesn't mean your mother didn't teach you what manhood was. You just departed from it, wouldn't you agree?
I don't know, maybe it sounds like I'm making a big thing over whether Audrey raised you into a man or not. But from hearing you I think maybe she did until you stopped listening. I hope I'm making sense in defence of your mother.

You still never answered why you cut your mum off from writing you. I would still like to understand that son. She never walked out on you, so why? Why did you stop talking to her? And why is it when you talk about her you sound as though you don't have much respect or love for her? Not judging, just saying how it sounds to me. Please explain if you don't mind, I would like to understand that.

Hope you're safe. Let's speak soon.

Errol

Errol,

No matter how I try break down the ting, you just don't get it. Manhood isn't something you can teach, it's something you do. It's like you're trying to play devil's advocate or some shit and I'm not with it bruv. Why ask me what's missing if when I tell you, you start question it?

You can make all the different scenario's you want. but as far as I know you're not a drug dealer and what I hear from you, you was a good pups to your older kids innit. Buying them bikes and shit, Mum had to make sacrifices to buy me stuff. Almost every gift came from a sacrifice. I'm just telling you I missed that balance.

You wanna know why I don't talk to my Mum? Maybe I'll get into that another time. It's kinda personal and I don't know what purpose telling you would solve. I'm out here trying to learn how not to hold a grudge against you. So ease off with the why I stopped talking to my Mum talk.

When I say I learned manhood from the streets it doesn't mean my Mum didn't teach me another form of manhood. All I'm saying is what my Mum taught me about manhood wasn't enough to prevent me from mis-learning manhood on the streets. This isn't a put down on my mum's part this is how I see it looking back.

Life in general is a test. And raising a son especially a black son in an area with hardly any tangible prospects or prominent male figures to look up to as role models is a test within itself. Not to mention the fact that the same area is known for low income, crime, police rivalry, inequality, broken homes, drugs, violence, and prostitution. The list goes on and will leave a young man with many unanswered questions about justice.

I wouldn't say I departed from what mum taught me, I'm just saying that I couldn't rely on only her teachings to help me survive growing up in this estate.

Mama Can't Raise No Man

I remember when one time I got robbed for my bike by some older guys from the area. I must of been eleven and these guys, fourteen. When I got home, Mum asked where my bike was and I told her it was one older called snatchers. She got on the phone and called the police, but she doesn't even like them. I told her not to but Mum weren't hearing it.

I was eleven and under mum's guidance, she gave a statement to the police. So the next day now, rumour was Snatchers and all his bredrins were coming down the school to do me damage. When dem man got hold of me - they started to call me a snitch. Then out of nowhere I see one older I looked up to from my block called PJ. He pulled up in his Audi TT and grabbed Snatchers and his boys. He broke it down for them. How can I be a snitch on road when I'm just a kid at school?! Then PJ told him to bring my bike back and to stop robbing yutes on the block or there'll be a bigger problem. Then he drove me home and told my Mum to drop the charges and even though she was reluctant to, she listened. That was one of the first times I remember realising that there is more than one way to deal with a situation and I felt that I couldn't always reley on my mum to know the best way to help me survive the reality of growing up where we did.

So what I'm saying Errol is simple in many cases I had to use my own eyes to guide me. No fault of her own, but Mum's vision was blurred.

Duane

P.S. You said I don't sound like I have respect for my mum. It may sound that way, but it's really not that. And if that's what reflects when I'm writing it's not intentional. And what you chatting about do I love my mum, how can you even ask me that? Kmt. Chat soon Errol.

Duane,

You know your problem? You too stubborn una. All you care about is the respect of the hood. Fuck the hood and fuck these youngers we need to get paid. I'm 25 G I gotta pay my bills like a real man should. And feds aint as bad as you make them out to be. You sound too much like your Uncle Leroy with all this Babylon talk. Police ain't pigs they shouldn't be disrespected like that either, it's these youngers on the streets that are the problem. I can't believe we was like them Duane we was lost. It sounds like you still think like a yute man. Or maybe you're jealous too, I hope not. Anyway it's not snitching if you're telling on your enemy. Last year you was on this you're done with the hood talk and now you wanna act like you're on this no snitching keeping it real talk. What's the hood ever done for us you said!

You need to stop acting up and come and take the jump. There's a job waiting for you and freedom if you wake up. The world's a dirty place bruv. Life ain't fair so I'm not playing fair either. So stop moving like a mitch on some quest for morals and justice and let's get this money M.O.E Money Over Everything just in a different way now.

Redz

Redz!

You've gone fucking mental? Really who are you? Do you think
this is some film. You mean to tell me you think it's ok to inform on
yutes? The same yutes we use to be. And you want me to join you
in making a living out of encouraging them to snitch on each other.
Nah G I can't jump that direction.

Tell you what though, don't write to me again. You sold your soul
to Babylon and the price was cheap. Don't worry about me being
jealous. I'd rather be dead broke than be a son of a snitch.
Next time you see man you better cross the road. I feel to move to
you on sight, and tump out your teeth but you aint worth the jail
time. Ex Gangster turned 'youth worker' and certified snitch yeah.
You aint no Ex Gangster bruv and you aint truly helping our young
lol. You're a fraud and a teef.

What Gangster shit have you ever done? You think I don't know
you lied about backing the beef against dem Hackney yutes back in
the day? Your own brother told me you snitched on Gary and Nev
from Tiverton - that's how you got your flat through that housing
association. Then you lied and tried to take credit for the money
ATM was sending me. I don't even know what to say to you. From
what I've said so far, you think I'm jealous? Delusion at it's finest.
I'm not the jealous type Redz and even if I tried to be I couldn't be
jealous of the man you think you've become.

I see you like some 21st century house slave... you know dem slaves
who shit on his niggas just to get a tinchy bit more comfy. Then look
down on the others. The sad thing is you can't even see it. You're a
man who's convinced himself of his own lies. The worst person you
can lie to is yourself bruh. Like I said don't write me again. I don't
fuck with your type.

We're done!

Duane

Duane,

You know what I'm gonna tell you sutten from now. I'm gonna tell you sutten now in pen and paper. There won't be no fighting going on you know. There won't be no fist-fight going on when you see me y'knah. Duane, someone will affi dead. I'm telling you that now. As a big man that fight talk shouldn't even come out your mouth. I'll get you killed Duane! I'll get you lick down. You will die, you will die!

Redz

Note to Prison officer.

"Can you block all letters from this dude please?"

Duane,

They have a saying that the apple don't fall far from the tree.

In the scriptures it says the Father is in me and I in him. He wasn't talking about a physical appearance. He was talking about his characteristics and the command that his father has given him. In order for man to know God was through Christ, they had to know God because Christ would demonstrate what his father's instructions were. If there is no father it doesn't mean that a child won't be like the father. Because you come from me, you're the seed of your father. And by the sound of it you have a lot of the same traits.

I bet if I met you in person you would recognise yourself in my ways. You might see the way I stand or some of the ways I think and say to yourself: Wow this man's just like me. We might find we have the same beliefs about women and our roles as men. There are certain behaviours and traits that I can see you get from me, like fearlessness, pride and independence. A seed yields a seed after its kind. That's how God created us.

There's another scripture that says: train up the child in the way he should go and when he's older he won't depart. Train means to teach and to show him and to point to him the way. So whatever way you train him that's the way he should go.

I spoke to Audrey the other day; she doesn't mind me sharing these thoughts with you. I asked her what she thought you kids missed by not having me around. Initially she felt "what they don't have they won't miss. What they don't have won't affect them." But then you started acting up. She saw in you my behaviour: the bad tempers, the constant arguing, the constant getting into trouble. The fruit (or man) really don't fall far from the tree. And that's what your Mum shared with me. This got me thinking. What really led you down the path you ended up on. Was it nature, nurture or both? I always wonder in the back of my mind.

Regardless of whether you and your Mother are on good terms

or not, she's still your Mother and from what I see that woman loves you more than you could ever imagine. She just might have a hard time showing it. But I bet a single day don't go by where she's thinking of you son trust me as a parent I know.

Keep your head up Duane you're not alone.

Errol (X?)

Errol,

With all due respect you can't chat shit and tell me my Mum loves me. What do you know? The reason I don't chat to my Mum is cos she rejected me. She kicked me out with nowhere to go at fifteen. I've been a teenager out here with nowhere to go.

How can a Mum do that? Where the fuck was I meant to live back then – man ain't priority on the housing list? I weren't even old enough to get on no housing list. What type of loving Mother doesn't worry about how her son's eating or how her son's sleeping? That's not love to me that's rejection.

And to top it off she only come to visit me once when I went jail for the first time. Not a letter nothing. You both rejected me. Mum just held out longer.

Mum never really gave me a foundation. It's like she use to preach to me telling me it's gonna be ten times harder for me to stand because of my colour. And then, she kicks me out her yard for occasionally bringing girls home and not being the example of a man she wanted to raise? Now, I don't have a place in society and I feel like I've just fallen into manhood by making mistakes instead of growing into it..

When I look around, it just seems that men in the hood, without dads seem to fall down a lot more than our sisters. Look how the media constantly portrays black men in a negative light. This is why it's so important that we have positive black male role models in our home. I chose to stay numb growing up because being numb is the only way I could get through. No one didn't teach me how to understand my emotions; my hurt or rejection. Looking back I feel like this was my biggest weakness.

Fatherhood was a struggle in the beginning. It's only now as a dad I'm coming to understand what it is I need to give to my kids as a man. I had many troubles learning fatherhood, Errol. When my son was younger I didn't feel it was normal to kiss him – not even goodnight. I never did all that hugging up stuff. I never see my Dad hug or kiss me goodnight so for me man don't do that. I never saw that shit at home or on Desmond's. So I believed men just don't do it.

But, when I hugged my daughter, I used to wonder if my son thought about why I never hugged him. I didn't want him to think I didn't love him. So I changed. I saw that feeling of hurt in my sons eyes and I never wanted him to feel as neglected as I did, so I fixed up.

You know what's funny Errol? Mum still tries to control me. One time sticks out: she said my kids didn't have the best future with an example like me. She was attacking me and my manhood. I told her in a firm voice that she ain't got no right to say negative things about my kids. Then she said "move from me" and pushed me as hard as she could and came in my face to do it again. So I grabbed her arms to stop her.

Mum called the police to kick me out of her yard. The same people she told me to watch out for. Errol, my heart nearly broke when I saw twenty plus officers with batons, shields out, and body armour in my mum's crib. What type of Mother does that; calls the police on their son when their son ain't a danger to them? What type of love is that? The way I saw it was she was vex, she couldn't control my words and she felt I outstayed my welcome.

Mum forgot the police weren't there to teach me respect, they were there to enforce the law (a law even she thinks is generally applied in a bias way). If they wrongly decided I did a crime, I would be prosecuted. Which means another conviction to add to my criminal record. My job progress would be hindered and it would be harder for me to provide a legitimate means for my children. Because of her actions, I would once again fall short of what the world defines as a real man. The same type of man she criticises me of not being.

I was so vex when she called feds Errol. On Monday Mum's shouting out Black Lives Matter and the next day she's acting like her son's life don't. Then she wants to write to me like everything's bless. Of course I love her still, she's my Mum but I can switch her off as easy as she can switch me off. It is what it is.

My Mum always taught me to be a man and take responsibility when I'm wrong. I can forgive Mum for anything cos that's my Mum. But she never takes responsibility and always puts ownership on me.

I don't care what no one says she was wrong for calling feds I didn't deserve that. She rather not talk to me than say sorry and you call that love?

Duane

Nephs,

I'm fed up. I'm done wid it. Vex. I'm vex you wouldn't believe bredrin. So hear what now I was walking with my new girl Kathy. You know, the one from up Plaistow? Well I was with her now and I did start notice when I'm walking street with her certain people start look pon me funny. Then imagine I'm walking down the high street when one pickey ed bwoy try barge past me, laugh, then shout out: "fake rasta."

I had to grips it up dread I don't business iyah, the yutes dem of today don't have no rarse manners dread. I grips him and tell him straight: "I'm not a rasta I'm a dreadlock." Yeah, bredrin. Tings nearly did get outta hand. But lucky for the boy I didn't have to use the drunken master on him. I'm done bredrin no more Mr Nice Dread. Make a man diss the I again and see if I don't box out him eye. I don't know why people can't just leff me alone.

Uncle Lee don't discriminate in the bedroom I love every colour in the rainbow bredrin. So what if I love my white women and the odd bacon roll. I still bun fire pon Babylon.

You see what nephew the way Babylon's got the human race ain't a joke y'nah. Hear my human race philosophy real quick. Imagine a race track with 4 lanes bredrin. Everyone's on the line ready for the 100m race of life. In this particular race you got the Black man lined up with the White Man the Black woman and the White woman. Before the gun pop off everyone's filled with enthusiasm and optimism. Then it starts. A quarter of the way down the line the White man and woman are neck and neck, joint first. While the Black man and woman are equal just behind. Then a quarter of the way down the line, tings change up. The White man's sitting in 1st place just about to win, while the White woman who is now in 2nd place ain't got a chance of catching him. Then struggling behind the white woman you got the Black sistren. She's had all type of obstacles getting in her way, and has been strong to overcome them to hold a third place. She aint got a chance of catching the white man, but she won't let anyone mek her feel that she can't win the race. But hear what now, she's so concerned for the Black man in

4th place that she can't run her own race properly. She don't want him to give up cos he favours her father, her brother, her partner and her son. She wants to see him winning.

The Black man's in last place coming up to 50meters, he wants to say fuck this. He's exhanusted tu-rarse, Babylon's drained him. He's tired of running a losing race but keeps his head high. The race is done now and 2nd place is no longer an option for the sistren. A part of the man wants his woman to win the race, while the other part of him was competing to show her that he's still a man. A part of the sistren feels frustrated that no matter how hard the Black man tries, the odds will always be stacked against him. Although she knows he had it harder than anyone else, at the same time she can't help but to look at him differently for taking so long to catch up.

You know how I see it neph, a women needs to understand that a black man has obstacles in front of him. It's not all peaches and cream. A brother and sister were not running in the same race. So when a sister finishes the race she can't be looking down on her man like: why is he taking so long to catch up. Sometimes a woman has to wait at the finish line and cheer her man on.

All I'm saying neph is we can't forget each others struggles. The sistrens' struggles are real and our struggle as brothers is real.

Walk safe me lion I hope you get your tag bredrin so you can finish this race as a man.

Uncle Leeroy

P.S Wille Lynch done told us from long time bredrin: Man against women, Dark against light, old against young the straight nose against the broad nose, the afro hair against the cooly hair. He knew what he was saying and wer're still facing the settings.

Aunty Jan,

Remember my little friend Anton who use to come round to mum's? Well he got shipped from Thameside to this prison and the guys who don't like me tried it with him.

When I was on the wing last week one brudder told ATM to go into his cell and get his jumper. I thought is this guy taking the piss? He's been preeing me my whole sentence, and he could see ATM is my boy. So I told him behave himself. True, this guy's a top don amongst his peers he thought he could bully up ATM like some boy. Anton stood up for himself, but I couldn't let no older man boy him off. So the brudder felt away cos I showed him up in front of his peeps. From then on the tension between us was heightened..

The respect that everyone else shows him, I'm not showing him, and that kinda got him vex still. Just because the brudder's in here on some M charge he's tryna go on like he runs the prison.

Every day I've come out my cell since last week, me and this same guy would bump into each other on the wing, he don't like me and I don't like him but I'm tryna behave cos I wanna come out of here. But every day I can feel this brudder and his little groupies giving me face and mumbling when I walk past.

So yesterday morning I'm walking down the hallway on the wing when this same brudder starts giving me more face but this time I couldn't help but look up. As I looked this dudes screwing me hard, so obviously I do the same, and keep walking towards my cell. All I could hear was this yute hyping outside with his bredrins: "Oi is my man Ricketts getting brave or sutten." So from then I knew it was gonna kick off but I've just gone in my cell and made myself a cuppa. Then out of nowhere him and his two bredrins barged in my cell. So I just stood up with my plastic knife behind my back asking man what they're doing in my cell. I was vex but didn't wanna act first, but he must of thought I was gonna be intimidated by a couple hench brudders standing in my cell.

When he saw I didn't give a f the man just walked back out with his two henchman and said come to my cell if you want beef my yute. But this guy was tryna run brain like I'm some eeediat. Like say I'm gonna go to his cell and move to him so the guvners can think I started it. He thought I didn't know how the jail ting run.

Anyway this morning, it did kick off. I saw my man in the holding cell with all of his boys dem. He walked up to me and said: "Yo Ricketts, what's with the bad man ting? I just stood there ready to defend myself and said: "You tell me! I think by the look on his face I embarrassed him in front of his homeboys. So he swang for me and missed. Then I gave him a one rarse lick then his boys tried to jump me but the guvners broke it up. He kept shouting your dead brudder. And I just shouted out: "everybody's a somebody you're not the only somebody!"

Anyway couple hours later few man from the wing came to my cell and said that they like the way I stood up to that brudder and that they didn't like him either. They said he thinks he's some super bad man that runs the jail cos nuff man show him ratings. I was shocked to see so many people didn't like him.

So now my man's vex. And I know this ain't over. The beef's still brewing now and it's defo gonna go down this time.

Duane

Hi Nephew,

Sorry to hear you're in a situation like this. And I'm happy you felt you could share it with me. But I've told you before and I'll tell you again:

You can't keep doing people damage in self defence for you or your little friend dem. cos it's only you getting extra time for that. And: "When you see your brother you got to try to see yourself." If you was looking at him like he was yourself what would you do to resolve this? If it was me in your shoes, I guess I would try make peace with the brother. But I know most men struggle with pride.

Anyway you make sure you walk safer than usual.

Love you Neph walk strong

Aunty Jan XXX

Duane,

Maybe your mum was scared you would hurt her. How do you know Audrey wasn't scared of you when she called police? Do you know what you look like when you get loud and angry? For all you know your Mum might think of the times me and her use to fight when she see's you get high rate. To be honest, I could tell Audrey was a bit intimidated by me even when I wasn't intentionally trying to intimidate her but she would never show me fear or back down. From everyting you say, it's like the cylce repeating itself. I for one know your mum hates the police so she must really have been scared that day. Not condoning it son, sorry Duane. Just asking you to put yourself in your Mum's shoes.

Errol

Hear what Errol,

You keep finding yourself calling me son. You better drop me out of that one there. And you know what else you can stop making excuses for my Mum. You don't know her. She ain't 'fraid of nothing or no one. There's got to be another reason, I mean who does that, really?

I mean how could the woman who raised me be scared of me? She's kicked me out her yard bare times. She turned her back on me by kicking me out when I was fifteen. And when I went jail for the first time the same year she never wrote me not once. You don't know about what me and my mum's been through so all this guessing is not getting us anywhere.

Is defending her your way of making it up to her for bussing out? Is that why you're making all these excuses for what she did? Personally I think she just didn't want me in her yard no more and she just used the argument as an excuse to get me out. She ain't scared of me bruv. Audrey's on this ting. She more serious than man locked up in here, you don't know my Mum bruv.

Just like with you, I don't know how to forgive her.

Duane

Sorry again for calling you son,

I really don't have the right after what I've done. Forgive me for forgetiing. I won't get into why your Mum called the police cause you obviously don't wanna hear it. What I will say is you'll never know if your Mum was scared unless you ask her. She's the person you need to talk to Duane. A mother can become scared of her son regardless of if she acts hard on the outside or not. At the end of the day you're physically a grown man now and when you're angry, that might be scary for her to see. But I'll leave it there.

As a person of faith, when I read your letters I see a conflict within you that is bigger than any individual conflicts you've encountered.

It's a spiritual conflict. It seems like you don't want to embrace God wholeheartedly. Maybe you're scared to put your trust in him but isn't it worth giving god a try? Maybe you will find the answers and peace you're looking for in God that you can't find in me, maybe not but why don't you at least give it a try.

Errol

Riss,

I guess the frustration for me is not feeling respected as a man by those I love. And no matter what I do for them it's never good enough. I'm forever falling short as a man and I'm tired now sis. I'm tired of being the man who fucks up all the time.

Duane

Duane,

I respect you as a man, but you need to respect yourself as a man. And that's when you'll see change. And you need to find the strength in you to want better for you. Because you value you. Looking at outsiders is not gonna help you, it just takes away your power.

Just remember bro we're both parents now, so we gotta do better.

Children begin an innocent bystanders to all our drama, but if we're not careful, they'll become a mess themselves. We need to stop blaming one another as man and woman, sister and brother. We need to come together as a community and change our perceptions. Change the way we react to each other. Change the way we feel about each other, and be more positive and encouraging.

Riss

P.S. You've been a man for years I've always seen it, you see it too. Love you to the bone bruh. Let me know if you're getting tag! Speak soon. X

Wha gwarn for you Errol?

Why you coming at me with all this God talk? I'm guessing you went church that day. Real talk though E 'llow the preaching. I mean... please

Like, with all due respect and that Errol, how you gonna read couple of my letters and claim say I'm at conflict with God? I talk to God sometime but he don't say nutten back. And don't worry, we can end the letters soon I'm just writing to kill time really before I'm back on road then we can go our separate ways. Minor.

Let's get back to the real issues. My only conflict and battle is between me the father, as a man. Me the son, as a man. Me the partner, as a man and me, the man who's trying not to behave or think like a road-man anymore. That's my battle Errol. So can we focus on that? If I wanted to hear about God all the time I wouldn't have put a ban on my Mum's letters would I?

Ever since you said Mum might have been scared of me I've been having flashbacks of bare other arguments we've had. Things did use to get a bit heated. She would say things to hurt me and on occasion I would do the same. I know where I get that mouth from.

One time when I first come out of prison me and mum was arguing, and she was shouting saying she didn't raise me like this. I asked who did and without hesitation she turned and said the streets raised you. She said "I don't know what you've become but I didn't raise that". She called me a "that!" - it hurt cos she meant it.

That day I didn't even argue I just kept thinking – if the streets raised me, where was you?

Duane

Duane,

I would say this to you, don't be hurt that Audrey said the streets raised you. You said you thought to yourself: if the streets raised you where was she? Well maybe she was able to be there for you physically but spiritually she was in her own wound, in her own pain. Maybe because of the pain she was feeling while raising you, she was damaging you.

Us as parents can't keep blaming our children when they've gone wayward. It doesn't matter how much kids a person has got, if we as parents are not spending time with you then how can we say we're raising you? We just feed you, wash you, put you to bed, but there's no interaction, there's no communication. There's no acknowledging. So you find that the children start to raise themselves, and they raise themselves in a wild way. It's either outside, with their mates, or elsewhere. Parenting is like gardening Duane, and when the garden's not kept, things get messy. Kept, meaning that you go out there every so often and you maintain it. You pull out the weeds, you prune whatever needs pruning, you make sure you plant whatever needs planting and when you plant, you make sure the seeds are getting enough sunlight. And if you leave that garden unattended for 3 weeks or so without taking care of business. When you go back out there it's as if you've never maintained it. And it's so easy for this to happen underneath a parent's nose.

Remember when you're a baby it's easier cos we feed change you then put you to bed. But as you grow with your own understanding and knowledge, that's when we need to become teachers. And if we haven't been taught anything about life how can we pass it on to you?

Obviously I can't say why your Mum kicked you out Duane because that's not for me to say. All I know from experience is some single parents have the skills to sit down with their children and talk when a problem arises. And some single parents will panic, and become afraid, and feel cornered. And instead of dealing with the situation they'll bury their head in the sand, or they'll go oldskool and fling the pickney dem out the house. Come out di house. Not because they don't love you but because they don't know how to deal with the situation, there's a fear of dealing with it. Why? Because she's not got the tools for when you became a teenager and are going into adulthood. As parenrts we we can only raise you to a certain point. So when you become a teenager we naturally start to panic and think: "Oh my God, Oh my God, they're answering back. Oh my God, Oh my God they're getting angry."

The parent or single parent starts thinking: "where yuh get so much brightness from? How you turn so brave? When you become so brainy? Who teach you?" Your Mum as a single parent is asking you these questions when she's not supposed to be asking you these questions. But because of a lack of knowledge and guidance on my part, you've had to go learn things your own way. And for that reason you should try not to resent your Mother in any way. The more you write me, the more I see where I slipped up as a parent. Through your letters I'm starting to see how hard it must be for any woman trying to raise a child alone. But like I said, because of lack of knowledge and teaching you've had to go and find your own way. I thank God that even in my absence you've managed to figure out some of the riddles of manhood.

Keep your head up.

Errol

Duane,

I've been speaking with Candy. We had a good little heart to heart
the other night. She admitted as to why you went missing on
the kids, why she stopped you from seeing them. She knows she
messed up and feels embarrassed for it. She said you can write to
the kids now and she won't ever come between you again.

I'm glad it's not true bro. You really don't need any more drama. You
just need to keep your head clear so you can come out early on
tag. Candy's still not ready to talk to you just yet, but she apologises
for going on the way she did. And says you can see the twins when
you come out. Oh and here's the new address for the kids:

251 Hollyfields Road, London

I saw the twins yesterday D, all I can say is you and Candy should
both be proud of yourselves. They are a reflection of you both and
have all your characteristics and such good manners.

I'm happy she saw sense before you came out. Now go write your
kids and we'll speak when you find out about early release.

Take care, love you bro.

Teah

P.S. I didn't get that job either. See it can be hard for a sister too, but
I won't give up like that. X

You know what T,

I've been thinking a lot lately. As mad as I am for Candy doing what she did, I can't stay mad at her forever. And I'm not condoning none of the fuckery she put me through with the twins neither. But I've finally realised some of the pain I caused. I betrayed her.

What I'm saying is I madded her with all my fuckery so I can't play the victim here. I was immature, and selfish. My wreckless behaviour could have messed up more than one woman in my actions. I can't bare to think of the other girls' heads I messed up on the way. I mean, I couldn't imagine anyone treating my babygirl, Justice, in the same way.

And you best believe I'm not raising my son to have bare gyal I'm gonna teach him better than that.

To say I'm grateful to be able to see my yutes when I come out is an understatement. Words can't explain. It's almost like it's not real, like it's too good to be true. I can't even find the words to write them right now. And I can't thank you enough sis. Just know I always got your back T, always. Tell Candy I said no hard feelings when I come out. Nuff Love .

Thanks for everything.

Duane

P.S. They said I could get tag so I should be out end of next month. See you when I land road! X

Errol,

You're right you know. I got bare passa going on round me right now. And a lot of it is my doing.

I've learned when you become a father everything we've learned about roadlife has to change. Cos if a man gets caught between being a roadman and a father he's gonna get caught in a storm.

My Aunty Jan told me that I cause a lot of my own drama and she's right. If I did what I was suppose to be doing I wouldn't be where I am now. God willing I won't be here for much longer; this place doesn't allow me to be the decent human being I can be. You have to switch into animal mode to survive. It's not my natural character to be this violent or hostile. But if you put me in a negative environment like the hood or prison and I can't talk my way out of it, then man stop talking.

I'm tired of beefing over petty shit. The who you screwings? Or the - you man aint from round here man-tality. Life is hard enough being a brother trying to pay the bills and raise a family — fuck beef. But that's the world I live in right now, so I'll always end up back in the storm when I'm in here.

Anyway forget all that Errol. Thanks for giving me the missing pieces to the puzzle of who I am. Just a few more questions before we can done this man-to-man interaction. What do you do? What are my other brother and sister like? Do you ever plan on telling them we exist?

Bless
Duane

P.S. You don't need to write me back to answer either. I've sent you a V.O so you can tell me face to face. Yeah, I feel like I need to meet you in person before we go our separate ways. So yeah, I guess I'll see you soon.

Hey Duane,

I got your Visiting Order last month but I didn't book it. I couldn't do it son. I can't face you. You might think I'm making excuses, but this is a lot deeper than I can explain.

From we first spoke I knew this was a bad idea. I just pray you don't hate me for what I've done now. I'm not the man you think I am. I'm going to stop writing you from today Duane.

I'm sorry son.

Errol,

You're a dodgy guy you know.

I was reading your letters and something didn't seem right.

Why you gonna write to me all this time then decide you're not willing to face me like a man? What the fuck sense does that make? And what's with all this I'm not the man you think I am talk? No disrespect and all that but I don't really rate you as a man anyway so it don't really matter what your secret is. You could be a cross-dresser for all I care; just don't come dress like a chick on a visit. Really though, how much more skeletons can a man have hanging in his closet?

What is it? You got more kids than you told me about? If that's your big secret I wouldn't hate you any more or less. Quite honestly Errol I wouldn't give a fuck.

I deserve to meet you in person. But I won't beg. I'm gonna send you one last V.O to come chat to me next week. If I don't see you when I come on the visit then I know what time it is.

Seriously, if you don't wanna come don't force it, but don't bother write me back with the bullshit, I beg. You're moving dodgy bare excuses (again!).

Duane

Hey guys,

Sorry you haven't heard from me in such a long time. It's been 7 months now. Daddy didn't want to keep writing you then stopping so I decided to wait 'till it's time to come home before you hear from me. And guess what Imarni and Justice? It's nearly time for Daddy to finish doing jail.

I only got 21 days left then you'll see me. That's 3 weeks guys! We can go cinema, play football, buy sweets whatever you like. Daddy's missing you guys bad, and I hope you're staying out of trouble too. No matter what happens I promise this will be over soon. I promise you'll see me next month before your 6th birthday.

Love you guys to the end of the world XX

Aunty Jan,

Hope you're good.

I've been keeping my head down reading couple of them books you sent me. The Malcolm X autobiography, and another one you sent, about that guy Tookie Williams, I'm rating highly. Anyway I've been seeing that same brother, the one I told you it nearly kicked off with. Him and his boys are still giving me the stale face looks. But it's cool though, next time I see him I'm gonna do the big-man ting and squash it. I don't want no drama with him and his boys.

Anyway AJ, I'm out soon. Thanks for the letters and wise words.

I'll come round for Sunday dinner when I get out next month. Love you Aunty Jan.

Duane

Duane,

I don't know how to tell you this but I got some terrible news bruv. Mum just had a heart attack this evening. She's in intensive. She's not stable bruv, I don't know how bad it is, call me when you get this.

I don't know what to do. What am I gonna do without Mum D?

Phone me A.S.A.P please.

Marissa

2 Months Later...

COURT TRANSCRIPT

Mr Ricketts, please stand.

On the 6th of July you were detained in
the segregation block of Swaleside Prison
following a fight that took place.
You later got charged with Murder. The
charges have subsequently changed to that of
manslaughter.

I have taken into account the circumstances
surrounding the incident and have come to the
conclusion that it was not one in which you
intentionally aggravated the deceased.

I have heard the witness accounts and I
commend you for your guilty plea on the
charge of manslaughter. One can only, and
wholly, sympathise with the recent revelation
of your personal connection to the deceased.
Nevertheless a sentence must be passed in the
court of law.

Mr Ricketts, you struck a single punch
of moderate force to the right cheek of
the deceased. The deceased collapsed to
the ground and died due to a subarachnoid

haemorrhage.

Staff at Swaleside have said you have become a man of good character. The sentence for an offence of this nature can be up to four years if there are aggravating circumstances. But I have decided to reduce it. Your sentence will be a further 18 months imprisonment. You will only have to serve 12 months of that. That is the sentence of the court.

Duane,

I know we've had a lot of drama over the last few years. We've both said and done things we don't mean, and we've both hurt each other in different ways. It doesn't matter who did what.

I want to say: I'm sorry. Stopping you from seeing your children was wrong. This isn't an excuse, but my head was all over the place. Please forgive me for that and let's try to give these kids something we didn't have.

Firstly, I was so sorry to hear about your Mum's heart attack. I took the kids down there to see her. The doctors say they're hopeful she'll recover.

And, I'm so so sorry to hear what happened between you and the other brother in there. Duane, that situation is a madness. I mean who would of thought? I can't imagine how you're coping with everything. Regardless of all the hell we've been through, you're still the father of my blessings. And you always will be. Even though I've let you go and I'm not in love with you no more – I've still got mad love for you and that ain't never gonna change. You're my twins' father, I see your face in them every day.

Don't worry about the kids I told them why you missed their birthday. I told them it's not your fault, but obviously I didn't give them the full 100.

I came down and watched you get sentenced at court today. I really hoped the worst wasn't gonna happen, but it did. Do not let this eat you up D, you're not a bad person. No matter what happens from here on I'll always let the kids know their Daddy is a good man.

Keep strong father of mine.

Candice X

Duane,

Bruv, I really don't know what to say to you. I'm so sorry D. First you're Mum, then this? When I heard the connection I was like rah that's a madness. It's not your fault what happened to the brother. Yes, you killed somebody by accident but you're not no murderer. Don't you ever make anyone tell you any different.

You shouldn't of even got time for manslaughter, anyone who was in court and heard evidence could clearly see that you were the trying to make peace for fuck sake and had no choice but to defend yourself. The law's a joke, I'm not even sure if I want to find work in this field anymore.

I've just watched the legal system send down a man for defending himself. That's not justice.

Please keep your head up bro no matter what they say we know you're an innocent man.

Praying for you

Teah X

Bruv,

I'm sorry about what happened. What can I say? I guess we both lost a brother that day.

I got some good news, Mum can come home. I'm so relieved I can't imagine what I would of done if... well it don't matter.

I haven't heard from you since I told you. I know you well enough now to know you didn't want to call me about Mum! I know I couldn't have that on my head if I was in there. Anyway thank God we're still fortunate enough to have her.

Mum told me she's gonna write you this week. I told her I'll do it for her but she's determined to find the strength to do it herself. She keeps saying she's not sure if you're gonna be able to forgive her this time round. God knows what she's on about. I think it's the medication and shock. But in advance I wanna say, don't hold any bitterness bro. No one is to blame for this. No one. Shit happens.

Love you bro my thoughts are with you.

Marissa X

Nephew,

My God I'm sorry. My condolences.

We don't control anyone's actions but our own. Your intentions in your actions were good when you approached that young brother for peace. You can't beat yourself up for what the overall outcome was. Just take this as a very harsh lesson to learn from.

Regardless of the extreme circumstances, I want you to know Aunty Jan is so proud of the man you have become. And I'm sure when you get out, with the new mindset you have, only love and prosperity will follow.

Remember Duane, the true path to enlightenment is internal. You have to learn to be kind to yourself before you can truly be kind to others.

Your barriers are there for a reason, cos they have protected you Duane. And they have helped you out growing up. But those defence mechanisms can constrict you, if you don't face them. The only way to overcome your demons is to realise that you've been hurt. And the only way to overcome that hurt is to drop your barriers and face your demons.

Cry if you can, and learn to love yourself.

Love you my nephew, you're a stronger man than you think.

Aunty Jan x

Son,

I'm so sorry for what I've done. I tried to tell you. I really tried. When you wrote me and said you didn't want any communication between us until you came out, I didn't know how to handle that. It hurt me that you wanted it that way, but I knew if I wanted to rebuild our relationship I had to humble myself and respect your decision.

Regardless, I worried about you. When you asked me to get an address for your Dad, I said I would. But the one promise I made to you wasn't mine to keep. I went to look for your Dad. I found him, I told him where you were, and what you wanted. The man said he couldn't bring himself to contact you.

When he said that my heart broke, I nearly killed him myself for denying you answers. Then Rissa told me you was asking her if I had sorted it. And I don't know why but I just felt that I needed to protect you somehow.

I panicked son.

I panicked and committed the biggest sin I have ever committed. I lied to you son. I deceived you. I'm so ashamed to write this on paper but all this time it wasn't your father writing to you - it was me.
In between letters I tried to tell you I swear. But as the letters got deeper it was harder to leave. I tried to see the positive in my actions but I couldn't. A sin is a sin. I tried to confess to you just after I sent the last letter. But the stress was killing me literally, to the point I dropped down with a heart attack thinking about what I'd done.

I never thought I was capable of such a thing. I've invaded your privacy on another level. I know all your feelings and thoughts about me, not having a father and what manhood means to you. I had no right to know that without you telling me.

If you never want to talk to me after this Duane, trust me, I will understand. But, I need you to understand, everything I said about me, I meant it.

No matter what I've done in the past I've always loved you. And the best decision I made was to keep you when I found out I was pregnant.

Love you son.

Please forgive yourself for my actions

Love you

Mum XXX

Duane,

I remember you running around in Toys R Us with your Mum and little sister. That was 20 years ago. I thought I would never see you guys again.

The next thing I know, I'm standing in court in a rage wanting to see the face of the man who killed my son. And I hear the judge say your name.

My soul was trembling. I turned my face with confusion to the docks to see the man responsible for the death of my son, was my son.

The worst thing is your Mum came to visit me a year and a half ago about you. She came to my yard and said you was in prison for the third time and that you needed me. She almost begged me to contact you and give you some closure. But I didn't care enough to act on it. I was too worried about my first born, Byron. He was in jail serving 15 years for a murder he committed when he was age 15.

I never thought about the possibility of you two actually crossing each others path.

Duane I'm sorry I walked out on you and your sister. I'm sorry for everything.

This is all my doing. Don't let the blood of your brother be on your conscience. This is all me. I bawl for Byron and I bawl for you, the son I walked out on. All this pain and confusion I've caused for not claiming what I made.

Byran never deserved to die and you don 't deserve the jail time. If anyone should be dead or in prison for this it should be me.

Lord God, I'm sorry son I'm sorry.

Errol

Errol,

It's nice to finally get the chance to write to you. Obviously I wish it wasn't under these circumstances.

When you left me as a child I was a confused boy. And as I grew I hid it and became a broken boy. And now with all this madness I've become a broken man. But don't worry Errol it won't last. I have faith my creator will help me put the broken pieces back together. I guess you wanna know what happened, how your son died I mean.

It was a week before my release and I was on the wing playing pool on the table. More time I'm in my cell, but I was anxious about getting out and I wanted to kill time. Byron and his bredrins came over to play as well. Anyway, one of them started hyping about it being his turn then Byron told him to allow it. Let them play first.

Me and Byron had already had beef brewing for a while, but up until now, it never went furrher than us just screwfacing each other. I thought O.K this guy is on the grown man business now. Maybe we can squash this. I leaned over the pool table picked up the stick and walked over to him. Then one hype bredrin of his got on the defence, like he thought I wanted violence. I turned to him and told him to cool himself, it's not that time but Byron's bredrin wasn't having that. Me and this guy had already had words over him disrespecting one young guy Anton who I've always looked out for.

Trust me Errol all I wanted to say to Byron was: "It's time to dead the beef and play a game of pool." But before I got the chance, his bredrin swang for me so I tumped him. Then I see Byron running towards me and I switched into survival mode and instinctively swang for him too.

When I hit him I felt my knuckles crack I hit him that hard. And the way he hit the floor...my God know man should never land that way. Everyone stopped fighting after that. No screws broke us up I think they was just as shocked as us. That's the story. I don't wanna hear I'm sorry from you, it's not gonna change anything.

If you want to apologise to someone, say sorry to my Mum and sister, they truly deserve it. I don't hold nothing against you though Errol. Maybe if you made contact it wouldn't of happened. Maybe we wouldn't be here but we are. Because of my actions my blood brother is dead, but because of your lack of action we didn't even know we were brothers. I'd rather not get to know you right now, maybe in due time.

I want you to let my older sister and my brothers Mum know how sorry I am. I hope you can be man enough to tell them who we are now. Other than that Errol I got no questions or hard feelings. Mum explained your absence and my brother's death confirmed it. I honestly hope you can live with yourself and find peace. I mean that. I've seen men break over less than what you're facing.

I forgive you Errol, because if I don't it will eat me up forever, and that's not a sentence I'm willing to live with. Try forgiving yourself Dad.

Duane

Neph,

How me see it, a mother can raise a son alone but with difficulty. When a woman interacts with her son, she displays her love, dicipline and guidance from the perspective of her feminie and motherly nature but she cannot play the father's role no matter how astute she is.

You see neph, in my opinion, she's not genetically or psychologically predisposed to do so. A woman can foster security and growth, give love and teach pricincples and do an outstanding job. But no matter how hard and well she does that job, her son can never become a man by imitating her alone and if there's no father around, the son's more likely to imitate what he see's on the streets or elsewhere, that mi nephew can be dangerous, your hear me?

The role of a father to me is to afford masculine nurture, emotional security, discipline, guidance, support and life's education from a male perspective. Much of this will be passed on through unspoken messages and observation.

What I'm saying here is simple. A son will learn how to become a man, in his mind, by observing his father, who is his first God. But if his father is not around, the other men in his life need to step up to the plate. We must go back to our African roots, cah it takes a viallage to raise a child. Ah dat mi ah say.

Now, solution time, what can we do to improve the situation? As black men and women we need to take a candid look at where we have gone wrong as individuals and as a collective. We need to evaluate the circumstances and environment which has helped to isolate our children, boys in particular. We can't engage in a blame game. But we can use our mistakes as lessons to go forward and improve our significant and highly important relationships. Ah dat mi ah say Duane Ricketts.

Black women must continue be strong but be weak at the same time. Just like us black men. They need us and we need them. Remember one hand cant clap!

I heard about the passa Duane and what it led to. What is done is done. Try know that your Uncle Leroy is proud of the man you're becoming. Your strength inspired me son. You brought your Uncs back from the dead. An addiction is a mistake repeated over and over again. And as hard as it was I had to give up my addictions. That's right D, I placed my last bet at the bookies last month and told Wray and his nephew we can't par no more, I don't wanna end up in a mad house with most of my bredrins dem.

Oh yeah and I've decided to stop sleeping round with this one and that one. Women deserve more respect than I was giving them.

Real talk nephew, don't follow my bad example with the women dem. Please I beg yuh, don't be like I was bredrin. Don't look pon women like a sexual object that you want to conquer. I've stopped all my free willie fuckries now. Don't get me wrong Neph, I still love up woman, yes, but I try do it with a little dignity and respect now.

Yeah dred, ah real ting dat. I can't hang out with Wray and his nephew again, dem man get me into too much fuckry rasta.

When time comes, I'm coming down to pick you up from the prison gate myself. I done told you already Neph – dem cyan't keep a good man down - freedom is a muss...

Lickle more mi lion. Stay away from Babylon, gyal and fuckry.
One love

Uncs

Mum,

I'm glad to hear you're well. Regardless of what's going on between us - I needed to hear that. Nobody's heard from me since this happened, but the real Errol.

Imagine where my head was when I heard the bad news about you. I had just come off the block for killing another brother by mistake. I walked in my cell and read a letter from Marrissa telling me you'd just had a heart attack, I just froze. I froze to the point where I forgot I just killed a man. Imagine, I was meant to be getting out the week after. It was like one big nightmare and I wanted to wake up. But I couldn't. When I went to court and the judge gave me my sentence for manslaughter I was still numb. When I came back I kept getting these letters from people saying sorry like they knew something I didn't.

Then one day I was in my cell and the real Errol wrote me a letter. And it hit me. I broke down crying, I've never cried so hard in my life Mum. I can't lie, you're right you've definitely betrayed my trust and deceived me. But it's O.K I get it.

Wow this is mad writing you. I feel like you know me differently now Mum and I feel like I understand you a bit better too. Believe it or not I found you impersonating my Dad easier to forgive than when you called police on me. But it's cool Mum I want to move on.

I couldn't forgive myself for what I've done over the years. And at first I couldn't forgive myself for killing this guy that ended up being my brother. I couldn't forgive Candy for not forgiving me for cheating. I couldn't forgive her for stopping me from seeing my kids. I couldn't forgive the system for the way they treat my people.

But I've learnt that in order to forgive others I have to be able to forgive myself. Forgiveness is everything. I'll keep working on not having any anger or bitterness in my heart towards anyone. Because in every adversity there is purpose and I get that now. Thank you for teaching me about the power of prayer. You taught me as a child that only God could judge me. Now I truly know what that means.

Love you Mum thanks for doing your best to raise me. I appreciate you. There wouldn't be a me without you. X

Acknowledgements and Thank yous

Acknowledgements

First and foremost I would like to thank the most high for allowing me to become the person i'm becoming in order to do what I need to do. For giving me the strength and endurance to overcome the MASSIVE trials tribulations and many adversities that tried to come between me starting and finishing the journey of writing and publishing, Mama Can't Raise No Man. For granting me with the gift of expression. Because the way I see it, if we are not allowed to express ourselves we might as well be dead.

Now, I wanna thank the people who helped me gain more of an insight on the subject at hand. Knowing me and my stubborn determination I would have done it with or without your help lol. But truth is I couldn't have done it to this level without your help and I'm grateful for the many hours of sitting down conversing with you guys about this real topic which helped open my eyes to so many different perspectives bigger than my own.

So in no special order I would like to individually say thank you to: Abby, Sandra, , Chloe, D-Lowe, Odz, Cell 22, Jade-Danny, Dan-Dan, Trim-Ting, Rickisha, Linda Mbagwu, Bagzy, Undiluted Expressions, My Barber Eddie, and all the mandem that reasoned with me in the barbers on the topic.

Thank you: Brother Jang-Jang, Iain Agar, James Beckles aka Becks, Adrian aka Kano, Khiry Ford (RIP), Kayley, Delroy-Lee, Wesley Travis, Kernal P, Taiti, Flava-W-T, Big John, Marine Lewis, Princess-Ma, Marce-Marcelous, Natasha Dougie, Cleopatra Rey, Winston Fowler, Sharon Mclean, Chemaine, Malachi Woodstock, Marsell, Jimil Sinclair.

Thanks to my power house sisters, Nena Nembhard, and Janelle Oswald. My bredrin Robert Rotibi. The Big man from the North West Harlesden — Rocky not forgetting Ricardo of course.

Thank you Samantha, Tara Young, Uncle Bonni, Mouse, Veronica Henriques, Vicki-Ann, Victor, Biko, Wale Raj, and Yamin, aka Yam Da Man. Thank you Carrol Thompson, and Dotun Adebayo I haven't forgotten our experience.

Special Thanks

In no particular order, a special thanks to: Lavern Ma, Aunty Carrol and Aunty Pam.

In the last few years I've gone to hell and back for various reasons. I can safely say that between these three women they wouldn't sleep too well if I didn't have a plate of food to eat or a roof over my head. These type of people are angels in disguise, Thank you.

Another special thanks to: Lez Quinn, Mark Prince, Rev Rose, Leslie Saunders, and again James Beckles. Without you guys, let's just say I doubt I would have been judged for the true person I am. Now I can continue the works I was put here to do. Thanks a billion times over.

I wanna thank all those people on social media who gave words of encouragement whenever I expressed giving up on completing this book, you know who you are.

Lyndon Walters, you know how we do Lyn. You may be the only person I know that I can call 24/7 around the clock. But that may be because you are the only man I know that don't really sleep. No, seriously our journey's been a mad one but that is for another book.

From the day you met me you've gone on and on telling me that I'm a genius who hasn't yet discovered his potential. I use to think this guy here is a mad man but it's finally hit home. I believe you when you say: "Talkers talk, tryers try, and doers do." I believe you when you said: "Potential + abilities = my capabilities."
And I believe you when you say: "Potential + Talent = GENIUS" (Lyndon Walters Upside down theory)
Anyway I give thanks for your life and our relationship. To cut it short King thanks for helping me discover the treasure within. Big up yourself Mr Walters - Aka Natty Lyn!

Special Thanks

Special, special thanks to Jassy - the mother of my blessings. Thank you for my children. Thank you for your patience you're determination, your encouragement and your brute direct honesty. Thank you for believing in what I bring to the table just overall a BIG thank you.

And to my children — Thank you, you guys are my reason for being a better individual. Daddy wouldn't be me without you. Every moment of time sacrificed I will make up to you. Love you eternally.

Last but definitely not least.

Mum,

I remember you telling me that you never heard me speak until the age of five. You told me that you were really getting worried that I had speech problems and that you was going to send me to speech therapy. Until one day you opened the bedroom door and heard me moaning to my older brother. You said the first words you heard me say was: "She's always making us tidy up, who does Mum think she is? The Queen of Sheeba?"

You said you wanted to give me some licks but you couldn't stop laughing. You told me you was so happy to know that I could talk that you let it slide that once.

I'll never forget the look on your face when I told you I'm writing a book called Mama Can't Raise No Man. It was a typical response of most single mothers I knew. I thought I was gonna get licks as a big man just for saying it. We sat down I interviewed you on the subject and we came to a similar conclusion.

I know we don't always see eye to eye. But that's OK. I still love you and understand you better than you understand yourself at times. I guess that connection we have was way more than cutting the umbilical cord could divide. You don't ever have to tell me to my face that you're proud. Because I know though our connection your bursting with pride.

No one on this earth can ever dare take credit for me being the author I'm becoming but you. You've been telling me from day when I was younger getting into fights at primary school that I need to write down how I feel. But I declined to do so.

You told me to write Prisoner To The Streets at the age of 15 and I declined because I didn't see the point of writing anything. You've helped raise a young boy into a man. But not only that you've birthed an author physically and literally speaking.

I could go on for days but I won't. Just want you to know you're still the Queen of my heart. And yes you're still my Queen of Sheeba! Keep fighting the good fight Mum. Try know I didn't get this strength and passion to influence others in this cold world but from you first.

Like Tupac said: "Aint a Woman alive that can take my mother's place."

How this book came to be published

The idea of Mama Can't Raise No Man and all the characters had been rattling around in my head for a while and I knew I had to get it all down on the page and write this book. I had decided that wherever I went my laptop must go with me so that everyday I could add to the story.

One day I was at my bredrin Crimson's place typing away when his friend Jason (Cuba) and his wife stopped in to check him. The brother Jason asked me what I was doing and I told him I was writing my second book. We caught a good vibe off each other straight away and he turned to me and said his wife Crystal was a publisher.

I didn't really appreciate that conversation at the time. But long story short things escalated and to me nothing short of divine intervention took place.

I found likeminded people who were ready to bring my work to the forefront. So on that note thanks to my big bro Crimson for unconsciously connecting the dots of destiny.

Thanks to my new big bro Jason for believing in me and for introducing me to Crystal and OWN IT! publishers.

Thank you ever so much to Crystal Mahey-Morgan for believing in me and having a mind and heart of gold so we can change the game.

The following poem is inspired by this novel and entitled:

Dear Mama, Dear Son

written by
Veronica Henriques

Dear Mama,

I'm sorry that I'm writing to you from behind bars.
I know all you ever wanted was for your son to aim high and reach
for the stars.

I am sorry that I ignored your guidance because I believed I was a
'big man'.
I'm now sat here feeling resentful and quite the opposite. A Juvenile,
with a small mind, in a small body shoved in a small cell with so
much room to know and so much room to grow.

I haven't even been in here long, yet I've had long enough to reflect.

I've had long enough to consider, to ponder, acknowledge and now
have deep regret.

On my first day I closed my eyes, opened them and blinked.

This was no joke, no dream..
My reality kicked in I think.

All I could hear was "Clink, Clink, Clink, Clink".
The prison guards keys locking me away, in the moment all I could
do was think.

I've become everything you tried to prevent me to be.
The Nucleus in cell, forming a basis of these brick walls which
builds something greater that I could not once see. Something
much bigger than me, happening in my society.

On observations of my internal surroundings, all I could see was
reflections of me.
Young, black and certainly not free !

I became the animal in a cage,
taking cold showers often filled with rage.
My food kicked over to me on a tray
the guards taking advantage because of my age.

In here....
I'm just a 'Bad Bwoy' who has no say.
Set amongst immature boy's fighting a war with no cause.
Big ego's, everyday seeking a round applause.

Oh Mamma,
I'm sorry I didn't try hard enough to listen to your advice.

I know I committed a crime which is a criminal offence,
but this is what I have to say to the judge in my defence.

You see...
I got caught up in the system as a result of being a victim.

My pain and my fear,
changed me into someone who didn't care.

My environment and my peer's taught me to love the roads more
than I loved myself.
I was blind but now I see,
a 'Prisoner To The Streets' no longer is me.

Mamma I can tell you now, this is a lesson learned.
I can honestly say when I leave, I will never return.

All I know is that I will continue to grow.
Your love and your guidance is needed you know!

Dear Son,

It's funny that you mentioned the guards do not have respect.
This all sounds too familiar however, your apology I accept.

I love you my darling, I truly do!
Whenever you need me I will be there for you.

Yes you're in prison and that is fact
But where you go from here will have more of an impact.

Your future is bright son that's all I ever wanted you to see
You can be as successful as you desire to be.

Yes I tried to prevent you from becoming another statistic in your
society.

They say 'Mama Can't Raise No Man',
to raise a man takes a community.

So I'm sorry that your writing to me from behind bars.
I know with you I tried and yes it's been hard.

But a man I believe and I know you will be.

One day you will return to the nest with your mind
and heart set free.

Because upon your reflection I can already see that you understand
the root of your problem is negativity.

So one day I'll stand an honoured and proud mum
because not all black youths who were in prison turn out to be
bums.

Yes son, my love and my guidance I shall give to you as tools
to help knock down those negative brick walls.

To free you from your pain and your fear
those heavy shackles that get you nowhere.

So ...

accept and embrace my tools as a positive intervention
because that growth that you mentioned?
They will surely help to get you there.

I love you my darling

More Books from OWN IT!

PRISONER TO THE STREETS
By Robyn Travis

PRISONER
TO
THE
STREETS

I learnt the hard way that you can't be *real* in something that's *fake* and you don't need walls around you to be IMPRISONED. This is the story of my life ON ROAD.

ROBYN TRAVIS

A real life account of Robyn Travis' journey to free himself from 'gang' life and 'postcode wars' in inner-city London to begin a new chapter.

NO PLACE TO CALL HOME
By JJ Bola

With colourful characters and luminous prose, this is a tale of belonging, identity and immigration, of hope and hopelessness, of loss – not by death, but by distance – and, by no means the least, of love.